The Birds,
Their Carols Raise

A Fictional Tribute to a Place of Warm Memories

In a Time of Volatile Change

Gary Brice

STEPHEN F. AUSTIN STATE UNIVERSITY PRESS 2017

For more information:
Stephen F. Austin State University Press
P.O. Box 13007 SFA Station
Nacogdoches, Texas 75962
sfapress@sfasu.edu
www.sfasu.edu/sfapress

Book design: Jerri Bourrous
Cover design: Jerri Bourrous
The cover photo pictures the author and his sister on a typical day in 1960.

Distributed by Texas A&M Consortium
www.tamupress.com

LIBRARY OF CONGRESS CATALOGING-IN-PUBLICATION DATA
Brice, Gary
The Birds, Their Carols Raise/Gary Brice

ISBN: 978-1-62288-162-8

This is my Father's world, the birds their carols raise,
The morning light, the lily white, declare their Maker's praise.
This is my Father's world: He shines in all that's fair;
In the rustling grass I hear him pass;
He speaks to me everywhere.
                    —Maltbie Davenport Babcock, "This Is My Father's World"

TABLE OF CONTENTS

AUGUST

THE WALK HOME

The sound of the street-sweeper rearranging the dirt on Park Street woke Kyle from his sleep. In his mind's eye, he saw the huge brush whirring through the gutters filled with dirt and leaves and candy wrappers. He opened one eye and watched the thundering machine pass, thinking that, one day, if he played his cards right, he too could run the street-sweeper over the streets of Nacogdoches.

He closed his eyes again and imagined the smiling children running after his machine; he could hear them shouting and see them wildly waving until he smiled and raised his hand in kindly benediction as he passed. When he drove the street-sweeper through the streets of Nacogdoches, he would not let his responsibility to the children be eclipsed by his work, though you could hardly call it work when all the children in town were envious of what you did.

Kyle turned and watched the sweeper come to the end of Park Street, turn right and disappear along the gutters of Lanana Street. From his perspective, it disappeared into another world. Just around that corner, just out of his sight, another world was waking as well. It was a world where poverty reigned, where laughter and smiles were a rare and precious currency, where the children watched the street sweeper pass without Kyle's thoughts of a brighter future.

As the street-sweeper did its job, dirt was expunged and broken beer bottles were whisked away. The roaring machine knew no distinction between White dirt and Black dirt, between the garbage left behind by affluence and the garbage left behind by deprivation. All it knew was that there was much to set straight on both streets. And there was also much to set straight in Nacogdoches, Texas, in those last months of 1960, and very shortly, Kyle Dexter would be both an unwilling participant in that change and an enchanted witness of it.

Kyle lay back on his pillow and felt the breeze caress his face and toss his hair. The huge attic fan down the hall (which had a blade the size of a B-24's propeller), was sucking in volumes of humid East Texas air through Kyle's open window and over his resting form. It was late August, but Kyle still felt deliciously cool as he pulled his bedspread to his neck and snuggled against his slightly damp pillow.

The birds were already busy celebrating another morning – the cardinal's familiar song, the chirping of the sparrows and the mockingbird's virtuoso performance. "The birds, their carols raise" was a line from one of the hymns often sung at First Christian Church, the church that sat not 50 feet from Kyle's home, the church that Kyle attended, and the church that was pastored by his father. And on this particular morning, the birds were raising their carols in splendid form.

As Kyle stretched beneath the covers, he tried to remember what day it was. He knew it wasn't the weekend, so there would be no binging on Saturday morning pancakes and no eye-searing marathon of cartoons; neither would there be a Sunday morning church service to wash and dress for.

Kyle smiled as he realized that it really didn't matter what day it was. He was delightfully adrift on the mirror-calm surface of a week in which there was not even a ripple of an obligation with his name on it.

Vacation Bible School had ended two weeks before and Kyle had the artwork to prove it, a picture of a sailboat made from brightly colored navy beans and brilliantly dyed rice, all tastefully glued to a rectangle of plywood. The masterpiece would sit on Kyle's dresser for a month until it was finally relegated to a remote corner of the attic where it would become a favorite among the appreciative roaches and mice.

And Little League had ended just the week before. Kyle's team, the Angels, had lost every game. Kyle had been the star pitcher for the Angels and had not only been instrumental in his team's 0-8 record, but he had also mightily contributed to the batting averages of dozens of his friends on the opposing teams.

But it had been a rewarding season nonetheless. Kyle's mother had attended every game, cheering her son on and rewarding every hit and every run scored with a package of baseball cards. Kyle had a cigar box filled when the season ended.

And school was not scheduled to start for another week which meant that the next 7 days were completely at Kyle's disposal. Kyle had thought about it carefully. Everyone knows that a week has 7 days, but only a few know that it also has 168 hours, and almost no one realizes that there are 10,080 precious minutes in that same week.

Kyle didn't want one of those minutes to pass in an ordinary way, in an unappreciated fashion. Each would be individually savored, contemplated, and enjoyed. No minute would be squandered; none would sneak by Kyle's watchful eye unengaged. Each would be awakened and prodded and wrestled into breathless submission until the week was finally spent, a fitting tribute to a summer fully enjoyed.

Kyle quickly dressed in his favorite pair of soft, well-worn jeans, his lace-up Keds and his prized Stephen F. Austin State College tee shirt that he would wear nonstop until his mother physically peeled it from his sweaty body and tossed it in the dirty clothes basket. He hurriedly bolted the cinnamon toast his mother had left for him, secretly resenting the three minutes that were drained from his hallowed store of 10,080. Still chewing the last bite, Kyle knocked on his sister's door to discover what adventures might await them.

Donna was 2 years older than Kyle and had left a trail of blessings for him at school. "You must be Donna's brother," the teachers would say with a smile. It was clear that she had done well in their classes and that they were expecting the same from Kyle.

Donna had long brown hair that was always pulled back in a ponytail. Always smiling, she was as outgoing and gregarious as Kyle was reserved and quiet. In fact, with Donna as his big sister, it was amazing that Kyle had learned to talk at all. With his sister by his side, he had precious little need to speak and only rare opportunities for doing so.

"Please come in," she said in her best theatrical voice. "We are pleased to be receiving visitors, even at such an ungodly hour." Kyle was used to Donna's histrionics, but he couldn't help but roll his eyes as he entered.

The "we," it turned out, was Donna and her best friend, Janette. They spent the night at each other's houses so often that a toothbrush with their name on it stayed in the other's bathroom.

"We're going to the library after breakfast if you want to go." Kyle did; in fact, he couldn't wait.

During the school year, the library at Raguet Elementary School satisfied Kyle and Donna's hunger for books. Twice each week, every classroom would line up and march to the library in order to return, check out, or simply peruse the hundreds of books that lined the library walls. Kyle loved those times and would slowly meander along the library aisles, fondly touching the old friends that he had checked out before, and dreamily considering the others that enticed him to do the same.

But during the summer months when the school library books were enjoying a much-deserved break, the old downtown Hoya Memorial Library was Kyle and Donna's second home. It was simply an old house (once owned by someone of historical import) that had been donated and restored by the city. It had a bronze plaque beside the front door, shelves instead of furniture, and lots and lots of books to choose from.

The three bibliophiles began the 15-minute walk to the library, down Mound Street, past First Christian Church, past the junior high that Kyle's brother attended and the high school that set beside it, and past the huge Indian burial mounds from which the street got its name.

The closer they got to the library, the more excited Kyle became. His stomach-dwelling butterflies stirred to life – just like when he stepped into the batter's box, just like when he waited for the nurse at the doctor's office to tell him it was his turn to get his polio shot. "Would it still be there?" he wondered as they opened the door and walked in. Kyle took a deep breath; it was! The magical library scent had not faded since his last visit. Kyle looked at Donna and noticed that she, too, was filling her lungs with the mesmerizing fragrance. Next to homemade bread and the scent of the Dexter house at Christmastime, there was none to match it.

The fragrance surrounded him as he opened a picture book on dinosaurs. The fragrance intoxicated him as he scanned a biography of Davy Crockett. The fragrance lifted him from the world of mundane things and transported him to another, brighter world as he looked at the brilliantly colored pictures in *The Wizard of Oz*.

If someone had told Kyle that his magical fragrance was, in fact, a blend of various molds and mildews combined with the smell of slowly decaying paper, he would have laughed in their face. He knew what the fragrance was – it was the scent of adventure, of courage and laughter and tears; it was the scent of imagination, the essence of truth, all blended and distilled and fermented in the minds and hearts of men and women, and at the proper moment, poured onto the pages of books. Each volume was a unique vintage, and every volume opened for the first time was as exciting as popping the cork from a prized bottle of wine.

Donna often checked out books that had only words, but Kyle was drawn to pictures, to images of swords clashing and salt spray filling the air, of bullets flying, stallions racing at dizzying speeds, wild animals in their habitats, and brave men defeating mythological creatures.

Kyle settled for a well-illustrated volume on Hercules. It was an old friend. He checked and found to his delight that his name was on the library card from the summer before. Kyle printed his name for what he realized might be the last time. Fourth grade was the season in which printing magically turned into cursive writing, and fourth grade was just a week away.

Donna and Janette each chose one of the Lassie titles. When they were finished, they would trade books with each other and get a two-for-one deal from a single library visit. With a relaxed afternoon of reading before them, the three bookworms headed home, but this time Donna, who was always looking for a new experience, led them along a different path.

Twelve-year-old Jasmine Washington was not having a good morning; furthermore, she had no inclination to believe that the afternoon would be any better. Her mother had gone to work and left her in charge of her sisters. Rosie was six and had a boundless supply of both energy and mischievousness. That, combined with a stubborn refusal to do anything her older sister said, meant that Jasmine would be averting disasters and extinguishing mischief for the entire day.

Lily was almost two, needed changing regularly and feeding often and required a watchful eye since she had a frightening disposition for ingesting anything that would fit in her mouth – dirt, plants, small toys, bugs, etc. When Jasmine wasn't corralling Rosie, she was prying open Lily's stubby fingers to find out what she had in mind for her next mid-morning snack.

This was not an unusual summer day for Jasmine. She had become a second mother to her two sisters since her father had left them in the spring. Cedrick Washington had been invited by a friend to help him take a truckload of chicken coops to Mexico. Upon arrival, Cedrick had discovered that liquor was cheap in Mexico and life there was slow.

He knew that when he returned to Nacogdoches, he would once again hear his wife complain about the power bill or the water bill or the rent; he would once again hear her whining about shoes and food and clothes for the girls. He would once again be reminded that he had no steady job and could not afford to lollygag around the house until he corrected that problem. When the coop truck returned to Nacogdoches, Cedrick was not on it.

Since that day, Mrs. Washington had worked as a maid five days a week to keep her family in food and clothes and under a roof that almost always kept them dry. On Mondays, Wednesdays, and Fridays she cooked and washed and ironed and cleaned for one family, and on Tuesdays and Thursdays she did the same for another. On Saturday she took care of her own home; Sunday was church day and her day to rest and be with her girls.

Jasmine was angry; she was angry that her father had left them and she was angry that her mother had to work so hard and so long and got so little for her labors. But it especially angered and humiliated her that her mother had to work for White folks.

Jasmine lived on the east side of Lanana Street. On her side of the street was an old cemetery, an old Negro church, and a half-dozen rent shacks, one of which Jasmine and her family occupied. The shacks were owned by a local banker, a White man who once a month ventured onto the wrong side of the street to collect his rent. He smiled in his wrinkled seersucker suit, and nodded with his panama hat in hand, and made reassuring promises when his renters mentioned busted pipes or dangerous wiring or rats, but nothing ever changed. Jasmine had long ago concluded that nothing ever would.

The other side of Lanana Street was another world. The west side of the street was lined with small modest homes, neatly fenced, flowers in the front beds and trees in the back yards. Each had a driveway and a car that left for work five days a week and once or twice for church on Sunday. In every one of those houses were White folks.

If there had been a line down the middle of Lanana Street with the words "Colored" on one side and "White Only" on the other, the division couldn't have been more obvious. It was Jasmine's lot in life to be consigned to one world yet to be so close to another that she could see her reflection in its shiny cars and smell its fried chicken every Sunday noon.

The August sun was blazing overhead. Jasmine sweated and yelled for Rosie to get back in the yard. She sweated and pried another pebble from Lily's filthy hand. She sweated and wiped her brow and looked down Lanana Street past the cemetery.

"What do you know," she said as she watched three children walking her way. "White children, and they on the wrong side of the street."

Donna was a great deal like her mother. If there was a new experience waiting, if there was the possibility of adventure, if there was a new and unexplored way of getting from point A to point B, both Donna and Mrs. Dexter would take it. And so when it was time to go home from the library, Donna never considered the utterly bland option of returning by the same route. "Let's take Lanana Street," she said, and her entourage willingly followed her lead.

When they came to the old Oakgrove Cemetery, Donna flew into her tour guide mode. "Ladies and gentlemen, if you will follow me into the historical Oakgrove Cemetery, you will discover where some very important dead people are buried!"

Donna effortlessly moved from one marker to another, commenting on each as if she had led the tour a hundred times, a commentary that made up with enthusiasm what it lacked in accuracy. Some of the symbols slowed her down a bit, but never stopped her. She was initially stumped by Masonic and Woodsmen of the World symbols, but she eventually explained them as college fraternities and moved on.

Finally, the lure of lunch and the promise of a lazy afternoon with a good book overwhelmed the three and they set out again down Lanana Street for home. Donna and Janette walked side by side, talking, with Kyle following in their wake.

Just when they were close enough to see Park Street up ahead, an adolescent Black girl stepped onto the sidewalk in front of them, crossed her arms, and waited. She was at least a head taller than Donna, was thin and wiry and wore a dress that she had outgrown months before. And she did not seem even remotely pleased to see the three children approaching.

Kyle saw that the sidewalk was blocked ahead and looked at Donna to judge the seriousness of the situation. He noticed that she was still talking and he was initially encouraged by the fact. But talking for Donna was like breathing; she could do them both when things were going well and when things were not.

Donna looked back at Kyle to make sure he was close. When she did, he saw the look of concern in her eyes. She continued to walk and talk until they could go no further.

"Hello," Donna said in her most disarming tone.

But Jasmine was in no mood to be won over. "What are you three doing on my sidewalk?"

It was more of a rhetorical question, but Donna never passed up an opportunity to talk. "We've just been to the library; our house is just around the corner."

"That should do it," Kyle thought. Donna had given the perfect explanation as to why the three were on that particular sidewalk at that particular moment. How could this young lady do anything but step aside and let them pass?

But stepping aside was not what Jasmine had in mind. In a heartbeat, Jasmine's world punctuated the world of the three. Without a word, she reached out and roughly took Donna's book from her arms. It was not a friendly act.

August in East Texas can be oppressively hot. The unobstructed sun was directly overhead and was at that very moment driving painters and construction workers and fishermen and gardeners into the soothing shade for a brief escape from the heat. Yet Kyle stood in the full sunlight shivering uncontrollably as he watched the confrontation before him. He shivered as Jasmine took Janette's book as well; he shivered as she glared at the three children and as she held one page in her fist, ready to tear it from the book, Kyle's teeth began to audibly chatter.

At that moment a car drove slowly by the children. Kyle looked to see if there might be someone he knew inside. There was not. Yet Donna, who would never let something as inconsequential as reality hold her back, saw the passing car as an opportunity for salvation.

Waving wildly and smiling broadly, Donna shouted so the whole neighborhood could hear, "Hey, Uncle Jack!" She continued to smile and wave as the car passed. Kyle and Donna did, in fact, have an Uncle Jack, but Kyle knew that he lived in Dallas, and he was almost positive that Uncle Jack wasn't driving on Lanana Street at that very moment.

Donna turned to look at Kyle. "That was Uncle Jack," she said, and Kyle, doing his best to play along, nodded weakly, visibly shivering from fear.

Donna had indirectly presented her case to Jasmine. *We are three inoffensive children walking home with library books, and we mean you no harm. Furthermore, we are close to home and have friends and relatives who will come out of the woodwork to assist us in our time of need as evidenced by the recent appearance of our Uncle Jack. You would be very wise to let us pass.*

Jasmine watched the car, hoping it would not stop and begin backing up. It did not. She looked again at the three children. When she saw the one in the rear, the small boy whose teeth were chattering, whose shaking form was wrapped around his library book, whose face was contorted in that familiar prelude to tears, Jasmine realized what she had done and what she was doing.

She had burned with anger when her own father had roughly mistreated Rosie, and she had burned with anger when he had stumbled home drunk and roughed up her mother. When Jasmine realized that she was doing the same to these three children, she was ashamed.

Without a word, Jasmine handed the books back to the girls and left the sidewalk. She found a stick and began to draw a hopscotch pattern in the red clay of her front yard. Rosie squealed with delight and began to bound from one square to the next. Lily watched her sisters jump, put a handful of sand in her mouth, and clapped her grimy hands in pure delight.

CATCHING THE BIG ONE

Pastor Donald Dexter took a break from his reading and looked out his office window onto Park Street. From his cushioned office chair he could see all the way down Park to its intersection with Lanana. He was especially interested in the view because it framed three children, two of which were his own.

The three walked together, one waved farewell at the intersection of Logansport, and then just his two made their way toward home. "Must have been to the library," he thought with great satisfaction. Their love for books was as much a family trait as Kyle's blue eyes or Donna's fine brown hair. He was pleased to have passed that love to another generation.

Pastor Dexter considered it a shame that the summer had flown by with so little time with the family. It would be only a week until school started and the family would be splintered in a dozen different directions: school, piano lessons, football practice, PTA, school plays, homework, Boy Scouts. He would hardly see them until the Thanksgiving break.

And it was especially a shame because Kyle had just had his ninth birthday and had received the gift he had asked for, a brand new Shakespeare rod and reel with a junior tackle box containing extra line, hooks, sinkers, corks, stringer, pliers, and one top water lure, a black Hula Popper, still in the box. In fact, everything was still in the original wrapping. They hadn't wet a hook since the day he blew out the candles.

Pastor Dexter was a very busy man. His church had over 250 members and many of them were elderly and required regular visits. At least two full days each week were spent on those visits and, in Donald Dexter's opinion, they were some of his favorite ministry moments. An unhurried cup of coffee with a saint who was a goldmine of memory and perspective, a casual walk through a pasture with a seasoned farmer, or the gift of vegetables fresh from the garden or of homemade mayhaw jelly. At least twice a year, Pastor Dexter was presented with a slice of unbelievably delicious black-bottom pie made with real whiskey. The white-haired widow who made the delicacy always smiled a mischievous smile when she reminded her pastor of the ingredients; "It's our little secret," she'd say. Moments like those helped transform his visitation days into times he would always cherish. But on occasion his devotion to his ministerial duties caused him to feel guilty about the time that was left for his family. This was one of those occasions.

"I could leave the office early today," he thought. "We could be at the Muckleroy's lake in 15 minutes. There's not a reason under heaven why we shouldn't," and he quickly rose to his feet to make the preparations.

As he did, he was just as quickly reminded of one good reason why he shouldn't. His lower back sent out a series of twinges that caused every muscle in his body to contract and his face to screw up in pain. He held to the side of his desk, shaking in pain. After a moment of stillness and some slow deep breaths, the pain subsided.

Donald Dexter was a Depression-era farm boy from the tiny farming community of Tyra, Texas, just a two-hour mule and wagon ride from Sulphur Springs, the small town which his brothers and sisters referred to as "the big city." He had known poverty and struggle all his young years. He wore one set of clothes the entire school year, received an orange or an apple each Christmas, never owned a bicycle until he was 15 and paid for it with his own paper route money, and often carried a syrup bucket with a turnip in it for his school lunch.

World War II was at a rolling boil when he graduated from high school, a feat that was made possible by the gracious dispensation of two teachers who felt sorry for the farm boy who was on his way to war.

At 18 he joined the Army Air Corps and became a waist gunner on a B-24 bomber. On his thirteenth mission, his plane was shot down over Italy and he experienced the unsolicited excitement of parachuting for the first time in his life.

At jump school, there was a poster that adorned the walls of every classroom, restroom, and mess hall. It portrayed a naïve corpsman parachuting to earth and landing with his legs straight; under the picture was the caption "NOT Like This!" When Donald Dexter landed in that Italian hayfield, it appeared that he did a perfect imitation of that naïve corpsman's landing, and as a result, his back was seriously injured in the jump.

For a year and a half, Don was a prisoner of the Germans in a POW camp on the Baltic Sea. By the time the Russians liberated the camp in the spring of 1945, he weighed just over a hundred pounds.

There was an unwritten understanding among G.I.s at the war's end. If you complained of a physical injury for which the government would be at all liable, it was assumed you would be hospitalized for treatment and kept in Europe for weeks or even months. But if you signed the release form that said you were A-OK, you were shipped home pronto.

With discs ruptured, vertebrae damaged, and his back in great pain, Don signed the release form to get back home to Texas and his family and his sweetheart, Vennie, who was waiting for him with open arms.

Fifteen years, countless letters to the Veteran's Administration, and three back surgeries later, Donald Dexter could still feel the pain of that inaugural parachute jump over Italy.

But pain or no pain, he went to the phone, called the Muckleroys for permission, and headed for the parsonage.

Kyle and Donna were sitting on the couch with their new library books looking every bit like someone who needed some exciting news.

"Get out of your nice clothes. We're going fishing!"

Donna, who did not care for worms, minnows, blood, or the smell of fish, decided to stay home and read. Kyle was a human tornado of activity until he stood breathless before his dad with gear in hand. A quick stop at the bait shop and they were on their way.

The Muckleroy's lake was actually a large stock pond, but it was lake enough for Kyle and his dad. Ten minutes and two dirt roads later, the two anglers parked the car and made their way on foot to the dam at the lake's end.

Mr. Dexter opened Kyle's junior tackle box and rigged his line with hook, sinker, and cork. As his dad squeezed the lead sinker around the line, Kyle had the uneasy feeling that he was being shod for battle.

He knew in that moment that he was taking one of those small, inevitable steps into manhood. Was he ready for the challenge? He was 9 years-old and had never caught a fish. Would that soon change?

There was a gnawing in the pit of Kyle's stomach as his dad reached into the minnow bucket and pulled out a big one. As he deftly hooked the minnow beneath its spine, Kyle was initially repulsed. But then he realized that this was simply one of the things that Fate had assigned for all men to do.

He readied his rig and hurled the bait as far as he could into the middle of the lake. The gauntlet had been cast. Now it was between the two of them – Kyle and the crafty fish. The battle of skill and patience had begun.

The cork set perfectly still in the water. Kyle waited a few minutes and then reeled it in a few feet and let the water grow still again. And then it happened. The cork began to gently, almost imperceptibly bob up and down. The bobbing grew stronger. Kyle's heart beat faster and his breathing deepened.

In another instant, the cork was jerked completely out of sight. The gauntlet had been taken up, the challenge accepted.

His father was as excited as Kyle was. Mr. Dexter laid down his own rod and reel and came to Kyle's side. "Reel him in, Kyle; reel him in," he said.

Kyle's hands froze with excitement; he simply couldn't crank the reel! It was then that Kyle demonstrated to his father a little-known but time-tested method for landing the big one. Kyle began to walk backward.

And as he did the fish got closer and closer to the shore. Kyle was literally going over the edge of the dam when the huge white perch on the end of his line became visible. From Kyle's perspective, she could have been a stunt double for Moby Dick.

One last big step down the other side of the dam and the huge fish was dragged onto dry land. The method had been unorthodox, but it had worked; he had landed the big one!

Mr. Dexter was beaming with pride. Kyle had done it. Their mutual triumph was complete.

And then – disaster! The huge fish gave a desperate flop and Kyle's line went limp. She was off the hook. With one flop and a flip, she was back in the shallows of the lake. Kyle stood motionless, helplessly watching the tragedy unfold.

But his dad did not stand by helplessly. Even as the fish hit the water, so did Pastor Dexter.

This man who had been shot down over Italy years earlier, whose back was a series of fusions and ruptures and pain, began throwing himself around like an adolescent gymnast in order to save Kyle's fish.

Waist deep in the water, placing himself between the fish and the lake, wildly slapping at the water with his cupped hands, he took on the aspect of a mythical hero in Kyle's childlike eyes. And like a story written for the Reader's Digest, the fish was thrown well onto land where she was recovered for the triumphal display at home later that evening.

Kyle's father, muddy and wet and hurting, had done what fathers have been called to do for their children since Adam held the infant Cain in his arms: he had sacrificed himself for the good of his child.

And like every decent father since, the joy in his eyes and the smile on his face revealed that it was a sacrifice he was pleased to make.

THE N-WORD

Tommy possibly had the largest head in all of Nacogdoches County. After seeing Tommy's head, Kyle had kept a running comparison between his and everyone else's, and no one even came close!

Not only did Tommy have a large head, but he had a pair of ears that stood at right angles to his head and made it seem even larger. And Tommy's haircut of choice was a "burr," a short, uniform cut that left the impression that in that place where ordinary people had a head, Tommy had instead a very large peach with ears.

Kyle was convinced that Tommy's head was large in order to accommodate all of his brains. He could speak quickly and fluently on any number of subjects; it seemed that any topic Kyle introduced, Tommy could expound upon with unhesitating certainty.

Take Indians, for instance. Kyle had mentioned seeing a picture of the great chief, Sitting Bull, in order to impress Tommy. Not only was Tommy not impressed, but the mention merely primed the pump for Tommy's exposition.

"Sitting Bull was the chief, but Crazy Horse was his field general. Custer had long blond hair. The Little Big Horn is actually the name of a river in Montana and Wyoming. Sitting Bull's tribe was the Sioux. Can you spell 'Sioux?' Most people can't. It's S-I-O-U-X. It's the only word in the world with three vowels right in a row." It would be years before Kyle realized that Tommy had fabricated that last bit of information, but by then, Tommy's reputation was firmly established.

Tommy lived only two blocks from Kyle and would often show up at his door ready to roam the neighborhood and enlighten Kyle with his stimulating commentary on all aspects of life.

It was the last Saturday before school started and Kyle was ready to fill the day to overflowing with fun and activity. He had been up since 6:30 and already enjoyed his mother's reliable and delicious Saturday morning fare – pancakes.

"Regular or wheat?" she had asked when Kyle drug himself into the kitchen. Kyle chose wheat pancakes, slathered them thoroughly with butter and buried them in Log Cabin Syrup that poured out of a real miniaturized log cabin-shaped container.

With his feast completed, he topped it off with a cold milk chaser. When the milk hit his stomach, Kyle had the feeling that he was carrying a bowling ball round in his gut, but he wouldn't have changed his Saturday morning breakfast for any other.

Checking *The Daily Sentinel*, Kyle discovered that the Kiddie Show at the Main Theatre was *The Beast from 20,000 Fathoms* with the main feature being *Watusi*. It would be a good day. There would be horror, gore, screaming ladies with some of their clothes torn off, African wildlife, evil natives and a king's treasure of gold and jewels. On top of that, there would be a couple of Three Stooges episodes (Kyle prayed they would have Curly and not Shemp) and at least a dozen cartoons. If a fellow watched the main feature twice (and Kyle almost always did), he could stay from 8:00 in the morning until 3:00 in the afternoon in that magical cinematic world of laughter and adventure.

And on Saturday morning, money would be no impediment. Friday night was when Kyle's dad passed out the weekly allowance, and he did it with theatrical flair!

Having served in the military, Staff Sergeant Dexter had not forgotten how he was paid, and he recreated the scenario for his children. On Friday evenings, Mr. Dexter would set up a card table, pile it high with coins, and sit behind it in a chair. If the young Dexters wanted their allowance, they knew the regimen to follow.

Ricky would step up to the table, snap to attention, salute, and say, "Sergeant Dexter reporting for pay, sir." The Paymaster would return the salute, count out Ricky's $1.25, pay him, and dismiss him.

Then Donna would repeat the scene. "Corporal Dexter reporting for pay, sir." Her dad would count out her $1.00, pay her, and dismiss her.

Finally, Kyle would go through the steps. "Private Dexter reporting for pay, sir." His salute would be returned, three quarters slipped across the table, and he was dismissed. What was commonplace and tedious in other households was high drama and highly anticipated in the Dexter home.

And Private Dexter could paint the town red with 75 cents! Admission to the movies was a quarter. Sugar Babies, Red Hots, and a Three Musketeers bar were a nickel each. Throw in 10 cents for a large Coke to wash it down with and Kyle was still left with 25 cents for comic books later in the day.

Kyle had been to the movies before, but always with a brother or sister to accompany him. On this particular Saturday, he would be walking to the movies alone. Tommy would meet him there, but Kyle was on his own to get his ticket and keep up with his change.

As Kyle approached the entrance to the Main Theater he noticed that the line was quite long. At least fifteen kids waited to pay for their tickets. But there was another ticket window! Had the other kids missed it? There was a lady sitting behind the window, just like the other booth, and the same admission prices were posted, just like the other booth. Kyle moved to the second window to pay for his ticket.

He not only felt like a grown-up, paying for his own ticket, but he also felt like a pretty clever grown-up for avoiding the longer line in favor of the shorter one. "One, please," he said as he slid his quarter toward the ticket lady.

But the lady's expression – her single raised eyebrow and her twisted-up mouth – did not confirm in Kyle's mind that she agreed with his "clever grown-up" label. Pushing the quarter back to him she said, with very little patience, "Honey, this is the Colored line; you'll need to get your ticket over there." She used her thumb to indicate the longer line.

Kyle, for the first time, realized that there were two lines, one that led White patrons downstairs to the main auditorium and one that led Black patrons upstairs to the balcony. Kyle's entrance led to nice seating, Sugar Babies, and clean restrooms. He wondered what the seating upstairs had to offer.

As Kyle took his quarter and moved to the other line, he noticed that Tommy was already there waiting for him. He had a crooked smile on his face, and when Kyle got close he laughed and said, "Were you standing in the N-line?"

Tommy said the word so freely, a word that had never been uttered in the Dexter home. And he sharpened it in his mouth between tongue and teeth so that it came forth with ragged edges. And he spewed it out as if it was leaving a bitter taste in his mouth and he couldn't get it out fast enough.

Tommy spoke the word like some of the soldiers in World War II movies said "Japs" or "Nazis," like it hurt them even to have to say the word, like it offended them even to have to admit the continuing existence of such people.

Kyle was confused and embarrassed and, like so many times in his life said nothing. Had he missed that word until now? Was it being spoken all around him without his awareness? Kyle began to think that was the case, especially as the events of the day played out.

Tommy was the kind of moviegoer who freely made comments during the movie. Pointing to the balcony he said, "That's where the N-s sit." For the first time, Kyle looked up into the balcony. It was filled with Black faces enjoying the movie just like the White faces below. He noticed that there were no visible stairs from the main floor to the balcony; it was only accessible through the Colored entrance.

At one point in the feature presentation, an African was speared in the throat by the evil witch doctor. Tommy quipped so that several rows could hear, "That's called an N-tonsillectomy." Quite a few giggled at Tommy's joke.

Tommy lived on the White side of Lanana Street. As he and Kyle walked home, he casually made reference to the other side of Lanana as "N-town".

Kyle walked the rest of the way home keenly aware that there were not just two admission lines for the Main Theatre, but there were also two admission lines for life: a White line and a Colored line, and they led to two very distinct realities.

Providence continued to make its point that afternoon. When Kyle arrived home, Ricky had just finished mowing the church yard for Sunday services. Holding up the mower blade that he had successfully removed, he informed Kyle, "Dad wants you to take this to Cason-Monk and get it sharpened. Tell them to charge it to First Christian Church."

Kyle knew the place; it was right on Main Street. Memories of the movies and of Tommy and of the two lines were very much in his thoughts as he walked into the hardware store. A lady walked toward him smiling.

"May I help you, young man?"

"I need to get this sharpened; it's a charge for First Christian Church."

"I'll go ahead and put that on your tab," she said. Kyle thought she was very lovely. "Just take it to Willie in the back and he can help you."

Kyle must have looked puzzled; he had no idea who "Willie-in-the-back" was and it must have shown.

"He's the N- in the back, sweetheart. He'll take care of you."

There it was again, and she said the word as naturally and as casually as if she had said "hammer" or "screwdriver." Kyle noticed that she didn't seem as lovely as she had when he first came in.

Kyle made his way to the back. It smelled of grease and gasoline and was filled with bins of screws and bolts and nails and assorted lawnmower parts. And slowly moving among all those parts was Willie.

Willie was an old, bent Black man with white hair showing beneath his Toro baseball cap. He picked up a screwdriver from the work bench and continued to make adjustments to a lawnmower's engine. Not knowing how to address him or what to say, Kyle simply moved until Willie was aware of his presence.

When Willie noticed the small boy he immediately rose to his feet and said, "Yez suh, how may I hep you, suh?"

Was it just Kyle's imagination or had Willie slightly bowed to him as he spoke? And had he called him "sir"?

"I need this sharpened," Kyle said as he handed the blade to Willie. "The lady up front charged it to First Christian Church."

Willie took the blade but kept his eyes lowered. "Yez suh," he said again, "I'll git a nice shap edge on dis heah blade." Willie fixed the blade in the grip of a large vice, took a huge metal file from the drawers beneath the workbench, and began scraping the dullness from the metal.

As he worked, a White man in oil-stained overalls came in the back entrance. He moved around the shop comfortably like one who worked there, saw the boy and Willie at work and said, "Willie helping you out there?"

Kyle answered, "Yes sir," and hoped the man wouldn't ask him anything else. The man spoke too loudly, and it seemed to Kyle that his broad smile was just a façade to cover something dark and sinister beneath.

"You helpin' this young man out, Willie?" he asked.

Willie nodded his head as he continued to work. "Yez suh, I'z puttin' a good edge—"

Before he could finish, the oily White man interrupted him, still loudly, but this time not bothering to hide what was boiling inside him.

"You look at me when you're talkin' to me, you hear me, boy!" He was talking to Willie, a man who was twice his age, and he was calling him "boy."

Willie immediately stopped his work, looked at the oily man, then lowered his eyes and said, "Yez suh, Mista Joe. I'z jus puttin' a good edge on the young man's blade."

Joe thought about the answer and said nothing for a terribly long time while Willie stayed virtually prostrate before him. Finally, looking at Kyle yet speaking to Willie, he said, "All right, then; you can git on back to work." Joe smiled at Kyle and winked.

Joe picked up what he had come for, winked at Kyle again, and left. Willie continued to file the lawnmower blade.

Joe had flexed his muscles for Kyle's benefit. He had snapped the whip and Willie had performed like a trained animal, and it had all been for Kyle's entertainment. Yet Kyle did not feel entertained; he did not feel like clapping for the center-ring revue. Instead, he felt sick and dirty inside.

As he watched Willie work, he realized that he had seen Willie's demeanor before. Kyle had been playing in the backyard once when a stray dog had wandered up. It was a small, short-haired mutt that was so skinny that Kyle could count its individual ribs.

Always an animal lover, Kyle immediately ran to the kitchen, opened the refrigerator and filled a bowl with anything he could find: leftover cornbread, black-eyed peas, rice, and white gravy. He ran to the stray dog and set it before him.

As the dog hungrily ate, Kyle reached down to pet him. But when the dog saw Kyle's hand near, he collapsed, first on his belly, and then rolled over onto his back in utter fear and submission. Kyle pulled his hand back and the dog rose to eat again.

Once more, Kyle reached forward and the dog groveled before him again. Kyle could only imagine the cruelty that had been inflicted on the dog that caused him to act so.

The bent back, the head hung low, those eyes cast down; all of that Kyle had seen in the abandoned dog, and all of that Kyle saw in Willie.

Willie finished his work, handed Kyle the sharpened blade, touched his cap and said, "Thank ya, suh."

Kyle wanted to tell Willie that there was nothing to fear from him, that he was not going to speak cruelly or act unkindly. But there was something in the bend of Willie's back and the whiteness of Willie's hair that told Kyle he would be wasting his breath.

Kyle lay on his bed that afternoon and stared at the ceiling. He thought about the two lines at the theater, about Tommy's jokes, about the oily White man's anger and about Willie. And as he did, other memories of the N-word and the mindset that fueled its use began to surface.

The year before, Kyle had been in Mrs. McHenry's class. It had not been a memorable year. She was old and stern and had a look and a voice that could turn a third grader's blood to ice. Students behaved for Mrs. McHenry, but not because they loved and respected her.

One part of the day that Mrs. McHenry seemed to enjoy above all the others was the half-hour immediately after lunch. After everyone was in their seats, she would take out an old cherished volume and read to the class. Kyle noticed that the pages of those books fell open and lay flat as if they had been read for decades to hundreds of children before him.

Kyle remembered how she smiled when she read the title, *Billy and the Major* by Emma Speed Sampson.

She read the Southern dialect with a familiar ease. She might have stumbled over it the first dozen or so times she read for her class, but by the time she read it for Kyle's class, she had it down.

As she read the first chapter, the word appeared. "I sho' do love n- chillun! When white chillun plays with n-s they knows how to give up — the n-s do, I mean. Wilkes Booth Lincoln an' me ain't had no fuss since we's born."

Several of the girls giggled at the mention of the word. Mrs. McHenry stopped reading and looked at the girls. Kyle's heart froze. He hated to see his peers disciplined and embarrassed in front of the class, but there appeared to be no way around it.

But Kyle was mistaken. Instead of scolding the girls for laughing at the word's mention, Mrs. McHenry looked at them and smiled an understanding smile, the smile of one who has met a kindred spirit, a smile of approval and encouragement.

The next time the word appeared, the giggles were more widespread. Mrs. McHenry seemed to become more animated and to work the audience with her dialect and clever mispronunciations of words, and when the N-word showed up, it was like the punch line to a joke that was a long time in coming. The class laughed heartily.

That year she read three books for the class: *Billy and the Major, Miss Minerva's Baby*, and *Mammy's White Folks*. Each of the titles was a cherished volume by Emma Speed Sampson and each was chock-full of references to N-s and N-babies.

Every day that year, Kyle heard the N-word enthusiastically used, and not by a friend who still didn't have all his permanent teeth or by an ignorant, angry, oily man, but by the one who was supposed to be in Kyle's life, the symbol of enlightenment and knowledge and truth.

Every day Kyle heard the N-word shamelessly used, and every day he came home to the nightly news reports of young Black men and women trying to sit at a lunch counter somewhere, or trying to register to vote or trying to go to the White man's schools.

Kyle watched the news and saw the neatly dressed, well-behaved Black people being yelled at and spit on and blasted with water hoses and chased by police dogs simply because they were not White. He heard the White people who were interviewed say that they didn't want N-s sitting next to their daughters in school.

That afternoon on his bed, as Kyle watched and as he listened and as he remembered, he understood. More completely than a myriad of politicians in Washington, the boy understood. Even though he was just a boy (or possibly, *because* he was just a boy), Kyle recognized the ignorance and the hatred and the fear that was behind every use of the N-word he had encountered. He did not yet know that a special blending of ignorance and hatred and fear, especially in the presence of social friction and high temperatures, results in an especially potent compound called Racial Unrest. But he and the town he loved and the nation he loved would become all too familiar with the concept as the years unfolded.

SEPTEMBER

FOURTH GRADE — FIRST DAY

Kyle was halfway through his first grade year at Mason Elementary School when his father accepted the invitation to be the pastor at First Christian Church in Nacogdoches.

Kyle's maternal grandfather had laughingly asked Kyle if he knew how to spell Nacogdoches. What elicited a chuckle from his grandfather was deadly serious to Kyle who barely knew how to pronounce the place where he was to live. He was months away from being able to spell it!

First grade is a formidable challenge for any young person, but to have to jump into an already established social network of six-year-olds can be overwhelming. But that was to be Kyle's destiny.

With unwritten charter, this group of twenty-two first graders had already firmly established what was funny and what was not, who was popular and who was not, what was allowed and what was not. To enter that society and disregard that unwritten charter would be social suicide.

A thousand questions flooded Kyle's mind as his mother drove him to Raguet Elementary School for the first time. How do you ask to go to the bathroom and where is it? Where do you sit to eat your lunch? How do you pay for it? What do you do with your tray when you are finished? Is it still two cents if you want an extra milk? What if someone can't spell "Raguet," much less "Nacogdoches"?

Mrs. Dexter walked Kyle to the end of the hall, the last room on the left, and was greeted by his new teacher, Mrs. Billingsley. She had already explained to the class that someone new was coming; they gathered behind her as a group to get their first look.

One little girl named Debbie spoke for the class. "Oh good, it's a boy; we need another boy!"

She had long braided pigtails, an ever-present smile, and dancing green eyes. Her smile and eyes would be directed at Kyle for years to come.

Debbie's gracious welcome almost quieted the agitated butterfly population in Kyle's gut, but not quite. Only moments after taking his seat he saw the posters of clocks on the bulletin board. One said 10:30 but Kyle only saw the numbers 1 through 12. Where did the 30 come from?

Then a sickening realization flooded Kyle's mind. Every one of his classmates, even the ones who were a bit slower than the others, knew what "10:30" meant. They were all ahead of Kyle. He had jumped into a race in last place, and he would never be able to catch up!

The butterflies in his stomach sounded the alarm and tears began to flow down Kyle's cheeks. Mrs. Billingsley kindly asked him what was wrong, and Kyle responded to her kindness by intentionally, knowingly and maliciously lying. "I have an earache," he said through his sobs.

Mrs. Billingsley had been teaching for many years and had seen such earaches before. As she led Kyle out the door to the nurse's office, Debbie was at her heels.

"What's wrong with the new boy?"

"He'll be all right," Mrs. Billingsley said. Kyle looked back, and even through his tears, could see that Debbie's smiling face had been transformed into one of tender concern. She continued to watch until they entered the nurse's office.

Debbie had known him for only one hour, and she was already concerned about his welfare. Kyle was greatly encouraged by the realization.

While his first day at Raguet Elementary was difficult, the days that followed were Halcyon days indeed. Within the first week, Kyle learned how to line up for lunch, how to buy extra milk and ice cream, and what part of the playground was reserved for Mrs. Billingsley's class at recess.

He also discovered that Mrs. Billingsley had put the clock posters up to cover a blank bulletin board and for no other reason. NO ONE knew what "10:30" meant! Kyle would survive after all.

Raguet Elementary was shaped like a large L. One leg was for grades 1-3 and the other was for grades 4-6. One was the "little kids" wing and the other was for "big kids." To move from one wing to the other was a rite of passage as worthy of celebration as a young Jewish boy's Bar Mitzvah or a young Masai warrior's first kill.

On the day Kyle entered the fourth grade, he would be officially a part of the "big kids" society. He would enter the realm of long division and cursive writing, of ink pens and homework, of safety patrol and flutophone lessons. In the world of academic pursuits, he would become a man.

Kyle and his mother walked together into Mrs. Hartsfield's room. And how aptly she was named! In her heart's garden, she cultivated and encouraged tender students until they were strong and vibrant and their veins flowed with the same love of learning that flowed through hers.

When Mrs. Hartsfield saw Kyle and his mother, she greeted them with exceptional enthusiasm. Kyle recognized her at once. She sat on the second row, left side of the First Christian Church choir loft. She knew Kyle already, and she expected great things from him.

The shortened day consisted of getting a locker assignment and a list of needed supplies. From there it was downtown to Stripling's Pharmacy where the supply list would be filled. It was controlled chaos when Kyle and his mom entered the drugstore. Students and their mothers were everywhere; each waited in line for the next available helper.

When it was Kyle's turn, Mrs. Dexter handed the list to the pharmacist who took an empty cigar box and began filling it with needed items: pencils, pens, erasers, glue, ruler, crayons, etc. When he came to "crayons" on the list, he asked Kyle's mother what count she preferred. She casually replied that the 24-count would be fine. In so doing, she inadvertently relegated Kyle to the lower echelons of budding fourth grade artists. He would have to struggle all year to move his way up.

Monday, September 5th, was Labor Day, but for Kyle and Donna, it was just one more day to endure before the exciting academic year began.

Kyle helped pass the time by examining his school supplies. He spread them across his bed and considered them one by one. The crayons were beautiful indeed! Each one was a brilliant color and each had a precise point and a delicious smell.

Those would be essential in completing the numerous mimeographed coloring sheets that would be passed out over the course of the school year. And Kyle could predict the order even before it happened.

In September, there would be one with a pile of school books and an apple and one with assorted fall leaves.

In October, there would be a glorious assortment of Halloween pictures to color – a black cat with its back raised (it was understood that the cat *had* to be colored black), a smiling jack-o-lantern, and a witch on a broom.

In November, the real celebration began. Pumpkins in a field with shocks of corn stalks tied in neat rows, a cornucopia overflowing with a bounty of good things to eat, a turkey with his tail feathers spread, and Pilgrims with heads bowed and hands folded sharing a Thanksgiving feast with their Indian neighbors.

If November was the dessert of the year, December was the ice cream and cherry that topped it off. There were coloring sheets galore: Santa Clause in full garb, a Christmas tree with a hundred lights and ornaments and dozens of presents beneath, stockings above a roaring fireplace, the Jolly Old Elf himself in full flight with sleigh and reindeer, and of course, the Nativity with all the actors in place and the Baby Jesus center stage.

A shipwrecked sailor could spend years on a desert island and have no concept of what time of year it was. But if he was transported to Raguet

Elementary School and spent a week in Mrs. Hartsfield's fourth grade class, he could determine by the coloring sheets alone the precise month and week.

Kyle gave his Crayolas one last sniff and closed the box. He didn't dare try out any of the crayons prematurely. They needed to be in perfect shape when he was called upon to use them in the days ahead.

Kyle put the box away and pulled out his Big Chief Tablet. The stern face of the Big Chief on the front was a reminder to Kyle that he would soon be called on to be a part of serious academic undertakings.

He opened the cover, held the tablet close to his face, and filled his lungs with its enticing fragrance. Kyle loved his Big Chief Tablet. Others would be drawn to more modern options, but Kyle loved the old reliable choice of his earlier years. Its pages were so clean and inviting.

In his second grade tablet, he had written and illustrated his favorite Robert Louis Stevenson poem, "The Cow." In practicing his presentation in front of his parents, he had reduced them to tears when he began, "The friendly cow, all red and white, I love with all my heart; he gives me cream, with all his might..." It was several minutes before Mrs. Dexter could stop laughing, compose herself, and inform Kyle that she was sure Mr. Stevenson had written, "*she* gives me cream" instead.

In the third grade, Kyle had written a three-page essay on the duckbill platypus, copied almost verbatim from the well-used set of World Book Encyclopedias that decorated the Dexter living room. He had been most proud of the effort.

What would the fourth grade hold? That was the magical Big Chief Tablet. Kyle could fill its pages with all sorts of brilliance and creative expression. What he filled those pages with could be the source of thoughtful delight for years to come.

And then it struck Kyle what the magic scent of the Big Chief Tablet actually was: it was potential! It was possibilities! It was nascent creativity! It was an invitation to greatness. Kyle carefully, tenderly closed the tablet and arranged his supplies in preparation for the day to come.

Tuesday was a blur of frenzied activity in the Dexter home. Donna almost cried having her long, tangled hair combed into a neat ponytail. Kyle couldn't find his new tennis shoes for the longest time. Mrs. Dexter was a whirlwind of activity, dressing two children for their first impression, and preparing a sack lunch for each of them. Kyle's lunch contained a bologna sandwich, a package of Hostess Cupcakes, a bag of Cheetos, a quartered apple and two cents for milk. He could have eaten for a week on that much food, but he didn't tell his mother. He could always use the leftovers to barter in the always exciting lunchtime exchange.

Mrs. Dexter waited in Raguet Elementary's semi-circular drive to drop off her payload. Buses were on one side, cars on the other. Several sixth graders were dressed in snappy white belts and carried bright red flags and were posted at the crosswalks.

"Flag out," the captain would say and the flags would be extended and provide a barrier of safety for pedestrian students. "Flag in" would halt the foot traffic and allow the cars and busses to move. There were many good things to look forward to at Raguet Elementary.

Kyle found Mrs. Hartsfield's room and looked around. Some faces were familiar, others were not. There was obviously a lot of paperwork to do and plenty of loose ends to tie up; Mrs. Hartsfield told the class to find a seat and talk quietly for the next hour. Kyle stayed quiet and tried to get a lay of the land.

Steve had a new flat-top haircut with lots of Butch Wax on it. He casually asked if anyone could spell Czechoslovakia. No one could. Steve promptly, and correctly, spelled it to the amazement of all.

Mark and Tom sat together. They had been friends since infancy and were inseparable. They were both busily drawing excellent Phoenician warships, their concave bows cutting through the Mediterranean waves. Kyle had not even heard of a Phoenician warship.

George made his way into the circle of learning. He promptly pulled out a wallet and displayed a real $100 bill. Kyle realized that he had entered the realm of important ideas and gifted people and that he would have to work hard to keep up.

Mozelle Hartsfield introduced herself. She told the class that, among other things, she had been bitten that very summer by a bat that came down her chimney and had to have rabies shots in her stomach. The class groaned at the thought.

She had also just completed a trip to Europe. She had traveled on an ocean liner that had its own swimming pool and had visited France and Italy, but she had especially loved France. She promptly sang "La Marseillaise" in French! The class was most impressed.

She reminded the class that there were books on the front shelves for those who finished their work early. Everyone was expected to stay busy and not waste a minute. There was also a tin filled with hundreds of cards on the front shelf; on one side was a question, and on the other side was the answer. "Quiz each other," she told the class, "until you know them all."

"Who wrote *Little Women*?" "Name the first five presidents of the United States." "Who was the discoverer of the South Pole?" "Name the 3 primary colors."

As the days passed, there would be an unofficial contest to see who could answer the most questions correctly before they were stumped. Mrs. Hartsfield had subtly ignited a fire in the minds of her students; learning, overnight, had become a passion and a joy.

Before the first day was out, Mrs. Hartsfield passed out the first of the mimeographed sheets that would be colored that year. It was the predictable assortment of fall leaves.

Benjie, a new boy, sniffed the sheet deeply and pretended to be drunk from the smell. Everyone laughed. They all knew the folklore that accompanied a still-wet mimeographed sheet. "One sniff: That smells good! Two sniffs: I feel dizzy. Three sniffs: I think I'm drunk!"

Benjie, on his first day, won the title of Class Clown, a title he successfully defended for the entire year.

As students pulled out their Crayola Crayons to color the picture, Kyle was brought to a sudden realization. Of all the boxes of crayons he saw across the room, the 24-count box was the smallest. Sure, it had the meat and potatoes of the color wheel, but a coloring sheet depicting fall leaves was not made for meat and potatoes.

All of Kyle's leaves were colored brown, red, or yellow. Other students glibly colored their leaves chestnut, sepia, salmon, maroon, yellow orange, raw sienna, or magenta. Several next to Kyle had the two-tiered, 48-count box and had more unused crayons than Kyle had in his entire box.

But that was only the middle-class box of the Crayola world! There were available, and Mark and Tom had them, boxes that had 64 crayons on three different tiers AND came with a built-in sharpener as well. Kyle could already imagine his efforts to accurately color the obligatory buckles on the hats and shoes of the soon-to-appear Pilgrims. Mark and Tom could pick bronze or goldenrod or copper or gold or silver; Kyle could only pick yellow from his scanty assortment.

And so the first day was complete. It had been filled with surprises, new challenges, and new thoughts. Mrs. Hartsfield had seen to that. Kyle was determined to master the tin box filled with knowledge, to make Mrs. Hartsfield proud of all that he accomplished under her guidance.

And new characters had been introduced into Kyle's life: wits and wise guys, reserved gentlemen and rowdy pranksters, flirtatious beauties and modest schoolgirls. Some would be friends for a season or two, move to other parts of the world and never be heard of again. Others would walk at Kyle's side for years to come, and as such, would become his friends for life.

WHAT COULD HAVE BEEN

Thursday had wound down until there was nothing left to do but lie in bed and listen to the radio. KEEE Radio, 1230 on the dial, was Nacogdoches' Top 40 station. The disc jockeys were funny, full of quips, wisecracks, and double entendres for most of the day. But at 10:00 a noticeable change took place.

It was 9:53. Kyle switched the radio on in the darkened room and watched the tubes glow brighter and brighter through the cracks in the back. Finally, when all the tubes were cooperating, the radio burst into song. Kyle heard the last strains of Marty Robbins' "El Paso" and then a string of commercials and political ads took the stage.

The five minutes of news, weather, and sports were only interesting to Kyle because there was a mention of the Lufkin vs. Nacogdoches football game that was scheduled for the following night. The two towns were only 16 miles apart and were part of a heated rivalry, the intensity of which was matched by the likes of Army vs. Navy, or Texas vs. Texas A&M. Everyone felt strongly about the rivalry, even Mr. Dexter. Whenever the Dexter vehicle passed through Lufkin, Mr. Dexter would roll down his window and spit. Kyle's mom would giggle and say, "Oh, Don," and that would be the end of it, but Kyle sensed some serious emotion in the gesture.

Almost everyone in town would make the trip to Lufkin on Friday night and stand and cheer and put their very hearts on the line for the love of the Nacogdoches Dragons. Even Kyle's class at school would enter into the excitement. On Friday afternoon, sixth graders would come to his classroom selling bright golden ribbons that had a picture of a Dragon breathing fire on a helpless Panther. It was only a nickel, so everyone bought one to remind themselves that Dragons Rule and Panthers Drool!

Kyle lay back on his pillow and contemplated the day to come. It would be Friday, which was a reason for celebration in itself. But in addition, the day would take on a festival atmosphere because of the Lufkin game that evening. Kyle was confident that no teacher in her right mind would try to introduce long division or the geography of the Great Lakes states, not on that day. Not only would there be a celebration at school, but there would be fish sticks in the school cafeteria and Kyle loved fish sticks. With only good things in the foreseeable future, Kyle laid his head on the cool pillow and listened to the radio.

It was 10:00 and he should already have been asleep, but he loved what happened to KEEE radio from 10 to 11 each night. For the next hour, there would be no car commercials or political ads, only quiet instrumental music and reflective thought.

The program began with 10 seconds of silence broken only by the barely perceptible sound of waves crashing on a distant shore. The breaking waves grew louder and louder and seagulls could be heard in the distance. Against this peaceful backdrop, the disc jockey began to read something profoundly beautiful. It began, "Go placidly amid the noise and haste, and remember what peace there may be in silence."

Kyle didn't know what the words meant, but it didn't matter. The disc jockey could have been reading the Nacogdoches phone book, but if he had done it with that voice and against that backdrop, Kyle would have felt as close to tears as he did at that moment.

The window at Kyle's head was open and the almost-cool September breeze stroked his face. Strains from "Ebb Tide" began to play and Kyle drifted off into that place reserved for fourth grade boys who have not yet known great sorrows, who are not yet burdened with great regrets.

And he would have slept the night through if it had not been for the car that slowly drove by his house, slowed under the single street light, and stopped. Kyle turned over to look at the clock; it was 1:30. The radio was hissing its monotonous hiss that would only stop when "The Star Spangled Banner" replaced it at 6 a.m.

Kyle switched the radio off and rolled onto his stomach and watched the street below him. He loved to be able to look out his second-story window and watch a world that had no idea that it was being watched. He loved to pretend that he was an American soldier hiding in a tall French barn and that the people below were Nazi soldiers who were trying to find him. They never did.

As Kyle watched in perfect silence, the driver's side door opened and a young man stepped out. He was wearing blue jeans and a black tee shirt. He gently closed his door, looked down the street in both directions, and made his way to the trunk and opened it. Before he took anything out, he looked around once more, but this time, his eyes passed over and then returned to the very window from which Kyle watched.

Kyle froze; his heart began to beat like a drum. Could the young man hear it? Could he see him in the window? But then Kyle relaxed; he remembered looking at his own darkened window from the perspective of the lighted street, and he knew that he was perfectly hidden.

The young man seemed content that he was unobserved. He took a bag from the trunk along with two large cans. Was it Kyle's imagination or did he close the trunk exactly like the mobsters he had just seen earlier that night on *The Untouchables*, with sinister stealth? Kyle watched him pass out of the streetlight's yellow cone and into the darkness, looking around him as he moved. Very strange, Kyle thought, very strange, and he turned over and went back to sleep.

When Kyle's mother called for him to get up the next morning, he noticed that the car was gone. Had he dreamed the entire incident or had it really happened?

Kyle slipped on his pants and made his way to the kitchen. He opened the cabinet door over the oven and saw that he had three cereal choices: Cheerios, Grapenuts (his mother's favorite) and a box of Raisin Bran that had been untouched for over a year. Kyle chose his favorite – Cheerios.

He took the box down and gave it a shake and listened. A second time he shook the box and listened. A casual observer would have imagined that he was simply determining how much cereal was left in the box, but Kyle had a more disturbing motive. He shook the box one last time and heard the sound of scurrying within.

Without alarm, Kyle took the flyswatter from on top the refrigerator, stepped outside onto the concrete patio, and carefully opened the Cheerios box. Laying it on its side, Kyle gave it a gentle kick and then another until the huge cockroach inside had had enough and tried to make a break for freedom. But the patio offered no hiding places and Kyle was a seasoned roacher. With one swat the intruder was no more.

Kyle pulled the package of Cheerios from the box to make sure there were no more surprises at the bottom; satisfied, he made his way back to the breakfast table.

As he ate his cereal, completely indifferent to the fact that another had been eating it only moments before, the phone rang.

Phone calls at 6:30 in the morning were unheard of in the Dexter home and could only mean bad news. Kyle and Mr. Dexter looked at each other and Mr. Dexter hurried to answer the phone. Kyle listened to the one-sided conversation.

"Hello"…"I'm fine."…"That's terrible!"…"Do they know who did it?" …"There might be some trouble at the game tonight."…"Okay, and thanks for calling."

Mr. Dexter went back to his paper and coffee but then looked up to see Kyle frozen, his spoonful of soggy Cheerios halfway to his mouth. "Well," Mr. Dexter said as he folded his paper, "you're going to find out anyway." Mr. Dexter folded his paper again, then unfolded it as he tried to decide how much to tell Kyle. "Somebody, probably from Lufkin, painted some bad words on the back of the high school building last night."

"Why do they think they were from Lufkin?"

"Well, they used purple paint, Lufkin's school colors, and of course, the game is tonight."

Kyle rinsed his bowl in the sink, went back to his room, lay on his bed and looked out the window. Puzzle pieces began to fall disturbingly into place. His heart began to pound; he began to sweat, even in the cool morning air; his skin began to tingle.

"Why didn't I see it?" he whispered to himself. "Who stops on Park Street at 1:30 in the morning? And the cans! Why didn't I realize that they were cans of paint? How could I have been so stupid? How could I have been so stupid?"

The potentially wonderfully day crept by in a deadened blur. The thrill of Friday, the ribbon sale, the fish sticks for lunch, everything, everything marched by to the tune of Kyle's newest refrain: "How could I have been so stupid".

The Dragons lost that night, 20-16, but the loss was just another unnoticed spoonful of darkness added to the overwhelming midnight in Kyle's soul.

Saturday was a beautiful day, but Kyle stayed in bed most of the time, lying on his stomach, looking out the window and imagining what could have been, what SHOULD have been! Over and over he played it out in his mind, watching it transpire in his vivid imagination.

It's 1:30 on Friday morning and a car stops on Park Street directly in front of the Dexter residence. Kyle's keen ears awaken him; like Tarzan, Kyle has learned that it is imperative to sleep with one eye open if you are going to survive in this world.

Kyle steadies his breathing, slows his heart rate and watches. "A black tee shirt – this is too easy," Kyle thinks. "The stranger is intending not to be seen; what mischief could he be up to?" Those cans! Kyle has seen cans that size before – paint cans!! And his movement in the direction of the high school…of course!

Kyle waits until the stranger passes into the darkness; then, like a whisper, he slips out of bed and down the stairs and into the night. He knows what to do. He has seen it done before. Moving to each tire, he unscrews the cap and bends the protruding tube. The air rushes out and the tire goes flat. The second, third, and fourth as well.

Then to the telephone for a call to the police. "I believe, if you circle the high school building, you will find that someone is up to some mischief." They don't believe him at first; he is, after all, only a child. They take too long to respond; the vandal returns to his car and finds that he cannot escape. The police finally arrive, arrest the man in black, and notice Kyle standing in his front yard, his arms crossed with satisfaction.

The next morning the Dexter household is awakened with phone calls and the sound of reporters knocking at the front door. The radio cannot stop announcing the good news: "Local Boy Nabs Lufkin Vandal."

Reporters ask their questions: "How did you know?" Kyle smiles and answers, "Wasn't it obvious? He just happened to stop on the wrong street." They are amazed at his humility, especially when he insists that his family should be included in any photographs for the newspaper.

At school, he is mobbed by admirers, even by fifth and sixth graders. Girls who have never before looked at him now want to sit with him at lunch. He is introduced at the halftime of the Lufkin/Nacogdoches football game that night. As he humbly walks to the middle of the field to receive a medal of commendation, both sides of the stadium rise to their feet in applause. He takes his seat in the stands with his family and hears the people whispering around him, "And he's only in the fourth grade!!"

The Saturday edition of The Daily Sentinel has Kyle's picture on the front page alongside a full-page story of his courage and quick thinking. It is organized in a whirl, but there is a parade through downtown Nacogdoches and Kyle rides high in a fire truck as the entire population of Nacogdoches turns out to see their hero.

He sees Betty and Debbie in the crowd. His gaze rests on them as on no others, and they feel his favor and they love him all the more because of it. And the crowd cheers and cheers and cheers.

The sound of the crowd died away in Kyle's imagination. The beautiful, beautiful picture of what could have been, of what SHOULD have been, faded away as well. All that Kyle saw was the harsh reality of the empty street before him.

Hours passed; daylight faded. The street was once again lit by the yellow cone of light. Kyle prayed that the clock would turn back 24 hours, just this once. Or if not that, he prayed that the stranger in black would return and try his mischief again. But even as he mouthed the words, he knew that the golden moment had passed and would never return.

A life-changing opportunity had passed him by and Kyle had not known to reach out and take it. The possibility of being admired and loved by everyone had been missed and was now gone forever. And Kyle, who desperately wanted to be loved, who needed to be loved, felt the regret more keenly than most. With a final thought of the parade that would never be, Kyle buried his face in his pillow and cried himself to sleep.

CHOOSING SIDES

The playground of Raguet Elementary School was a vast, sunny field marked by four or five ancient sycamore trees. "Field" is probably a poor choice of words since it usually implies some form of vegetation. But years of tag and red rover and football had reduced this particular field to acres of hard-packed red clay. A million waiting footfalls dared any bit of foolish flora to lift its head above ground, and the few surviving blades of grass that took the dare were in distant corners of the yard, isolated areas that were completely disdained by the ravaging hordes.

The school itself made up one side of an enormous rectangle; the other three sides consisted of what seemed like miles of hurricane fencing. In later decades, the fence would be seen as necessary to keep kidnappers, child molesters, and other perverse types away from the school children. But in this more innocent day, it was seen as necessary to keep the swarm of wild school children from harrying and molesting the benign and unsuspecting members of the local community.

At exactly 2:00 p.m., a bell rang and a dozen doors burst open and the quiet, deserted field was transformed instantaneously into a confusion of noise and movement. But in a heartbeat, the confusion became order. A dozen separate groups went to their own predetermined portion of real estate and began the most anticipated hour of the day – recess.

The girls from Kyle's class were already amusing themselves with a jump rope and assorted counting rhymes. He noted how smoothly and painlessly they began their hour of play. The boys, on the other hand, had formed themselves into a loose circle, a milling, pulsating blob of energy and anticipation. Once again, that timeless, nauseating ritual leading up to recess was about to begin – choosing sides!

Even though Kyle could hold his own in the world of academia, on the playground he was short and slight and easy to overlook, and choosing sides was always a potential opportunity for humiliation and self-scorn.

It was Friday, and that meant free play, and free play in fourth grade always meant kickball. The team captains were chosen by Mrs. Hartsfield, and they were always the same – Benjie Pearson and someone else, but always Benjie Pearson.

Benjie may have paid homage to subjects and predicates during third period, and he may have bowed the knee to states and capitols after lunch, but at the end of the day, when the classroom doors flew open, Benjie was Lord of the Playground and every minstrel lay was sung to him.

If you had asked Kyle why he admired Benjie, he would not have been able to tell you. The reasons were either too ethereal or too embarrassing. What was it about Benjie that caused teachers and students alike to admire him? His good looks? His raspy voice? His bright eyes? His tanned face? His immaculately combed hair? His swagger? Or was it his boldness that bordered on bravado?

All those went into the pot, but for Kyle, there was an additional reason for his admiration that he had never mentioned to anyone: Benjie could sweat like a horse! While a soaking wet shirt and a dripping brow might disgust society's more squeamish members, it was to Kyle the soggy badge of courage, masculinity, and athleticism.

By contrast, Kyle seemed completely incapable of breaking into a sweat himself. He could sprint from one end of the playground to the other on a hot fall day, feel his brow for the results and draw back nothing. Benjie, on the other hand, could break into a sweat doing long division.

How often had he heard the teachers sing the praises of Benjie and others with words like, "Oh my, you boys are a sweaty mess!" Once Kyle had proudly walked beneath the teacher's gaze having played as hard as anyone else only to hear her say, "Didn't you get to play today, Kyle?"

And while Benjie alone could be the Sultan of Sweat, Kyle often dreamed that one day he might at least become the Prince of Perspiration.

So, of course, Benjie would be a captain. It was only right that he should be. Wiping from his brow the sweat caused by intense contemplation, Benjie glanced over the group of non-captains and considered his first choice. Some of the boys were bouncing up and down with their hands in the air shouting, "Benjie, Benjie!"

Kyle watched with embarrassment their degrading, fawning efforts to be chosen even though it meant wallowing in the red clay at Benjie's feet, even though it meant tossing aside every shred of pride. And with his compassionate heart, Kyle pitied them. Besides, it didn't work; Kyle had tried begging and bouncing for a full week without noticeably moving up a single notch in the talent depth chart.

And so Kyle waited silently with the masses in the ranks of the unchosen, secretly making promises to God about all he would do or never do again if only He would spare him the shame of being chosen last.

Dan Williamson, who could kick the ball a mile, was chosen first. He showed no emotion; he expected to be chosen first. Then came Mike Haas, another heavy hitter; Mark Nichols and John Woods followed.

After four or five choices, the natural athletes were all gone, and so another, stranger economy began to work in deciding who would be chosen next. Had someone brought cookies from home and shared them over lunch? Had someone's dad just gotten a new car? Was there a birthday party or a sleepover coming up soon? Had someone laughed with hearty enthusiasm at one of the captain's jokes or helped him with his math homework? All those intangibles were stirred into the stew as the captains made their final choices.

Mark Wilson and Tom Taylor never played on opposing sides. Benjie took them both, giving Sam Medley, the other captain, the next two choices. Steve Johnston, whose dad was the basketball coach at the local university, knew the rules to every sport. And since it was sometimes to your advantage to have the official interpreter of the rules on your side, he and Henry Spies went to Sam's team.

The next two choices were Jerry Easterly, who could do more chin-ups than anyone in the school, and George Middlebrook, who, when his full name was employed (George Frederick Middlebrook, the Third), had the longest name in Christendom.

Now only four remained: Tom Pruitt, David DeGrand, Richard Burgess, Jr., and Kyle. As there were not two ounces of athletic ability among the four of them, other reasons dictated the order. Benjie had played pool at David's house the weekend before; David ran to join his team. Tom's older brother drove Sam's school bus. Suddenly only two were left.

But Richard Burgess, Jr. had three obvious strikes against him. First, he went by all three names. Secondly, he had recently moved from a town called Waskom that no one had ever heard of (and several openly doubted the existence of. And finally, to top it off, he wore his hair much shorter than the style of the day dictated. Kyle should have been a shoo-in for the next choice.

But Richard also had a major advantage that had just been revealed the day before. His mother had come to school to pick him up for a dentist appointment and she was a knockout! And all the boys had noticed, Benjie even pretending to faint in the presence of such beauty. Richard was chosen next.

As Kyle trotted to the other team, he felt the blood surge through his cheeks and ears as he endured the shame, not of being chosen last, but of not being chosen at all. On that particular day, everyone else had been tossed a lifeline that dragged them from the fearful waves of slight regard and rejection. Kyle, on the other hand, had been forced to drag himself into the lifeboat since its occupants were too busy celebrating their own recent salvation to offer any help.

Kyle wondered if God had not been impressed with his efforts to barter. Or possibly, he reasoned, the other boys had far more heinous offenses with which to negotiate and thus secure the favor of God. Either way, Kyle had once again come in dead last.

As the teams took to the field, Kyle kicked himself for actually showing up for school that day. He could have faked an earache and watched sitcoms and quiz shows all day. He should have had the decency to spare his team captain the shame of actually having to include the name of Kyle Dexter on his team roster. But instead, he had selfishly chosen to go to school and inflict his miserable self on the ranks of the gifted, the qualified, and the worthy. And now he must pay for his decision.

As the game progressed, Kyle noticed with what abandon the chosen players played. Whether they struck out, popped up or kicked a homerun seemed no longer to be of any consequence to them. To his amazement, he realized that it no longer mattered because *they had been chosen.*

They were no longer part of that miserable society whose members know self-worth based only on their performance for that particular day. They were now free to enjoy the game from the perspective of The Preferred. After all, when the dust of the day settled, the others could still reassure themselves that *they had been chosen.*

Kyle, on the other hand, had everything to prove. He flung himself after kicked balls, ran the bases with a crazed determination, and even sprinkled water from the drinking fountain on his brow to give himself the appearance of sweating. All this he did knowing that his place among his friends hinged entirely on what he did and that his status in their eyes rose and fell with the passing of each out and every inning. Unlike the others, Kyle no longer had the luxury of simply being; he had to do and do well all that he did so as to gain the approval of the chosen.

Another bell rang. Kyle and the others lined up to go back to their classrooms. Had he done enough to avoid last place the next time teams were chosen?

If only he had called the police when he saw that car parked outside his window. If he had made that one decision, he would have assured himself of being chosen first for years to come.

"Being chosen first," Kyle mused, "Now that would be something."

THE TOUCH OF GOD

Bus 93 rolled slowly along Lanana Street. It was 4:30 in the afternoon and the few children left on the bus seemed to be drained of the boundless energy they showed when they boarded nine hours earlier.

The bus was one of the oldest in the fleet. It had been a bright, shiny yellow when it made its maiden voyage fifteen years before, but the hot East Texas sun and several thousand trips along the red dirt back roads of Nacogdoches County had scoured the shine clean off.

But even though the outside of the bus was faded and dreary, the inside was bright and cheery and Pastor Noah made sure it stayed that way. Noah Starr had been the pastor of Zion Hill Baptist Church for twenty-five years. He and his wife, Esther, had raised their three children in the church and seen them grow up, marry, and move off to greener pastures. But Noah and Esther were not alone; every new school year brought forty bright-eyed passengers for Pastor Noah's bus and forty smiling faces into Noah and Esther's lives.

Noah had driven Bus 93 since it was new, and he had promised God that he would make it a safe and pleasant place for the children who rode it.

"Lord," he had promised, "You know better than I do that these little lambs have a hard row to hoe with not enough to eat at home, no decent clothes to wear in public, liquor-drinkin' daddies, and overworked mommas. Lord, if you give me breath each day and a voice to speak, I will be your voice crying out in their Wilderness of Pain. I will personally apply the Balm of Gilead to their wounded souls and speak Your blessing over them daily jes' as long as I hear your say-so, Lord; jes' as long as I hear your say-so. Amen."

And Pastor Noah had been good to his word. Riding #93 had become a bus-riding adventure for the past fifteen years. Every child who stepped onto his bus had been prepped by someone older and wiser. "That is Pastor Noah's bus," parents and older siblings had warned, "And you are a blessed child to be on it this year. But if you talk back or misbehave or disrespect his bus, he will put you out for the week and you will be walking your feet off. Do you understand me?" They did.

As each child stepped on the bus in the morning, they became part of a firmly established ritual. Pastor Noah placed his big hand on the head of the little ones and took the hands of the older ones and said the same to each of them. "This is the day the Lord has made; we will rejoice and be glad in it. Am I right?" Each responded with, "Yes, Pastor Noah," and took their seat for the ride to school.

Other buses had seats covered with black vinyl, cracked and ripped, the yellow foam stuffing spilling out, and the springs visible and sometimes painfully exposed. But not in Pastor Noah's bus. Esther had made seat covers for the past ten years so that each seat was covered with a bright and cheerful pattern. Church members had given her yards and yards of leftover material, and as soon as one seat became worn or tattered, it was covered by one of Esther's creations of love. No two seats looked alike, and children hurried to the bus when school was out to sit on the seat with their favorite pattern.

"That old vinyl sticks to your sweaty skin in the hot days and makes you shiver like you're fevered in the cold days. The seat covers are no trouble," she told anyone who asked. "All the seats are the same size. I've done it so many times that I could cut out the pattern and sew it together with my eyes closed. It's the least I can do for those babies."

While he drove, Pastor Noah kept one eye on the road and the other eye on the large rearview mirror. He could see every child on his bus and every child could see that Pastor Noah was seeing them. He had not had to pull the bus over to discipline a rowdy passenger in over ten years. At school, the children on his bus heard tales of unconcerned bus drivers and all sorts of misbehavior and mischief in the other buses, and they were very glad to be riding with Pastor Noah.

What started with the Psalms of David in the morning ended with the Books of Moses in the afternoon. As each child stepped off his bus, Pastor Noah spoke a blessing after them. "The Lord bless you and keep you," he would say as the bus rolled to a stop. "The Lord make His face shine upon you and be gracious unto you," he added as the door opened and the children stepped out. "The Lord lift up His countenance upon you," the door closed, "And give you His peace." The bus rolled on to the next stop.

Every child heard that ancient blessing spoken over them as they left the bus. Most heard and felt honored by the pronouncement, but some heard with calloused hearts and painful memories and bleak futures, and wished the old man would simply shut up.

Bus 93 slowed to a stop on Lanana Street, its worn brakes squealing the announcement that children were almost home. Mothers heard the squealing, opened screen doors, and stepped onto porches when the announcement was made. The school day was officially over, and the evening at home was about to begin.

Jasmine Washington was the last passenger on the bus and knew her stop was next. She gathered her books, stood, and held onto the seat in front of her until the bus had stopped. "The Lord bless you and keep you." Jasmine walked down the aisle and kept her eyes from Pastor Noah's. "The Lord make His face shine upon you and be gracious unto you." Jasmine stepped off the bus and saw her overworked mother standing on the porch of the unpainted shack. Her ever-present anger began to approach the boiling point.

Sometimes it frightened Jasmine when she felt her anger approach the point of no return; other times, she just didn't care. And on this particular day, she just didn't care.

"The Lord lift up His countenance upon you and give you His peace." Jasmine stopped, wheeled around, and glared into Pastor Noah's eyes and the cauldron of her anger boiled over. For months it had been licked by the flames of injustice, disappointment, hopelessness, abandonment, poverty, and humiliation, until there was no place for her anger to go but out.

With her eyes squinted and her facial muscles drawn tight, Jasmine spoke in a low, cold tone so that only Pastor Noah could hear. "I don't need your stupid blessing, old man." Her volcanic anger was erupting and no power on Earth could stop the destructive, burning flow. "You don't know me, and you don't know my life, and you don't know jack squat about Peace. So keep it to yourself!"

And then she knew it. In a few beats of Jasmine's heart, she had ruined her life forever. The words that felt so deliciously satisfying as they spewed forth now struck horror into her heart. What had she done? She had spoken back to Pastor Noah; she had even said "jack squat" to him. Jasmine had no idea what it meant, but she had heard the words used by those boys in her neighborhood that her mother told her to stay away from, so she knew it was nothing good.

And her mother! Her mother would be devastated when she received the report of what her oldest daughter had said. And others would hear as well. And her mother would be whispered about, and snickered about, and shamed by her friends and fellow church members. Jasmine shuddered at the realization of what she had done and stoically waited for Pastor Noah to respond in kind.

But Jasmine saw no anger in Pastor Noah's face because there was no anger to be seen. "You're right, child," he said calmly and quietly so that only she could hear. "I don't know your life, and I don't know what waits for you inside that door." He was looking at the front door of her house.

"And you're right again that I don't know much about peace in this life, but one thing I do know – there's Someone who knows everything there is to know about you, and all He knows about you only makes Him love you more. He's the Prince of Peace, child. Anytime the load of this life gets too heavy, He'll carry it for you. He knows all there is to know about peace, child, and He just happens to be my best friend!"

Pastor Noah smiled and Jasmine's eyes grew wild with disbelief and confusion. He pulled the lever and the doors to the bus began to close; then they opened again just as abruptly. Pastor Noah had something else to say. "The peace of God be on you just the same, Jasmine." The doors closed and the old bus slowly moved away. And he had called her by name.

As the dust and the diesel fumes died away, Jasmine turned and walked toward her home. "What was Pastor Noah saying to you?" her mother asked. Jasmine kept her eyes straight ahead and in that adolescent tone that every parent fears and every child eventually adopts, she said, "Nothin' important."

Alone on Bus 93, Pastor Noah was visibly excited. He shifted the gears with enthusiasm and opened the door of the moving bus just to feel the breeze on his face. "Yes, Lord," he said in his strong pulpit voice, "I see it clearly, Lord. I'm still here on this green Earth, still drawin' breath and drivin' this here bus for little ones like her. Break her anger, Lord; let the waves of her malice crash on the Rock that is higher than I. Transform the water of her rage into the sweet vintage of love."

Pastor Noah was too excited to sit. He stood and kept his foot on the accelerator. Bus 93 flew down the highway. "Hallelujah," he called out the open window. "You got room for one more in ol' Noah's ark, Lord?" Laughing and crying at the same time, he sat again and slowed the bus as he neared his home, tears streaming down his wrinkled cheeks. "There's always room for one more in your ark, Lord; always room for one more."

Jasmine opened the screen door. Rosie was sitting at the rickety dinner table cutting out dolls and dresses from a *McCall's* magazine. Miss Boatwright, one of the ladies Jasmine's mother cleaned for, kept a *McCall's* magazine prominently displayed on the coffee table in her living room. When the most recent issue arrived, the outdated one was given to Mrs. Washington to take home to her girls.

In each *McCall's* issue, there was one page designed for a young girl with scissors. It featured Betsy McCall, a smiling, round-faced girl who wore only her underwear. But that was no problem since each issue also featured clothes and accessories that could be cut out to make Betsy more presentable.

Rosie had a shoebox filled with Betsy McCall dolls, clothes, and accessories. The August issue featured "Betsy McCall Visits Pollyanna" and included turn-of-the-century dresses and hats.

Rosie carefully moved the blunt-nosed scissors around a frilly dress, watchful not to cut off the tabs that would hold the dress on Betsy's shoulders. Her lips puckered and curled with every careful move of the scissors around the paper dress. She was far too busy to notice Jasmine's arrival from school.

While Rosie worked with scissors, Lily sat on the floor playing with her spools. She had a cigar box filled with empty spools, some that Rosie had colored with her crayons, others with eyes and smiles that Jasmine had designed.

Lily could play for hours with her spools, stacking them, rolling them, talking to them, and playing "house" with them. She too was much too busy with her spool family to notice Jasmine's arrival at home.

But Jasmine changed that in an instant.

Jasmine intentionally let the screen door slam as she walked into her house. To do so was to show blatant disregard for one of the very few rules Mrs. Washington required her daughters to respect. "Close the screen door quietly," she had said a hundred times.

Not only did Jasmine let the screen door slam, but she had thrown it open as far as the tired, rusty spring would allow it to go. "If I'm going to transgress," she reasoned to herself, "I might as well do so wholeheartedly."

The screen door stayed wide open and unmoving for a brief moment until the ancient spring finally remembered to do its only job. As the spring contracted, the door moved faster and faster until it slammed with the report of a shotgun.

Rosie jerked at the sound and snipped off the entire top of Betsy McCall's party dress, tabs included. "Jazzie!" she screamed in anger.

Lily was startled as well and knocked her neatly arranged spools into chaos. She began to cry as she surveyed the devastation that had befallen her spool family.

Jasmine was the cause of the tears and the devastation. On the one hand she felt guilty and ashamed for what she had done, but on the other hand, she was glad that everyone knew that, on this particular evening, she was in no mood to be trifled with.

"Jasmine Louise Washington," her mother whispered to herself as she followed her firstborn into the house. "What's come over you, child?"

Mrs. Washington was a student of many things, but human behavior was her specialty, her own daughters' above all others. She knew that there are battles that need to be fought and conflicts that need to be engaged in.

She was also well aware that there are times to avoid conflict, that there are battles that fight themselves and struggles that would eventually collapse under the weight of their own foolishness. "No point in raking leaves in a windstorm," her mother used to say. Mrs. Washington comforted Lily and went to the kitchen to start supper.

There would be collard greens from the fence row in the back yard, boiled noodles, cornbread, and fried bologna for supper. Not a lot of fried chicken, pork chops, or roast and potatoes were cooking on the east side of Lanana Street that night.

Jasmine dropped her books on the dinner table and went to the kitchen faucet for a drink of water. She let the tap water run for a moment until the rusty orange liquid became almost clear. She placed her hand under the running water and drank deeply as the water pooled there.

Jasmine rubbed her wet hand on her forehead and over the back of her neck. September might bring cool weather to children in sixth grade readers, but in Nacogdoches, it was still as hot as blazes and it would stay that way for several weeks to come.

Jasmine knew the routine. Homework, help with supper, get Rosie and Lily ready for bed, and lay out clothes for the next day. Only when all this was completed was she allowed a few minutes to herself to read or think or relax.

Jasmine took her books to the bedroom and sat on her side of the twin bed she shared with Rosie. There was an invisible line that passed down the center; Rosie Territory was on one side and Jasmine Territory was on the other. The line had been disputed, battles had been fought, and blood had been shed to win the uneasy peace that existed when the sisters were in bed together. And one stray toe over the line could at any time render the armistice moot.

But Jasmine was alone for the moment. She laid out her school books on the bed and contemplated the work that lay before her. For Math, she had a "Multiplication by Ten" worksheet to complete. It would take her all of five minutes to do. She also had a chapter in her American Geography text to read. It was titled "America Before Columbus" and featured a map of the North American continent as it appeared before the European settlers had arrived.

The book itself was titled *Sea to Shining Sea* and the cover ordinarily featured pictures of the Grand Canyon, a vast herd of buffalos on the plains, and ocean waves breaking against a rocky shore. But Jasmine's textbook had no such cover. In fact, it had no cover at all.

The distribution of textbooks worked the same way every year. The pile of available texts sat in the front of the classroom. The teacher would call a name. That student would go forward and select a text, give the number to the teacher, and be seated. Joshua Anderson always got first choice and Homer Williams was always the last to choose. Jasmine was next to last.

By the time she and Homer picked a textbook, all the books with covers were gone. "It has the same words as the ones with covers," her mother told her, but her mother's wisdom fell on deaf ears. It was a seemingly small inequity but it reminded Jasmine of the greater inequity that filled her every day, and the sting and the shame of that injustice glowed red hot every time she lifted her worthless, godforsaken textbook to read.

Jasmine set aside her homework when her mother called her to help with supper. As she arranged the plates and forks and jelly jars on the table, Jasmine knew her mother was stealthily watching her, looking for clues that might explain her anger. "Let her wonder," Jasmine whispered to herself.

Dinner was finished and the dishes cleared away. And through it all Jasmine never said a word, not "Thanks for supper, Momma," nor "Pass the butter, please," nor "May I have some more milk?" Jasmine let the minutes pass in a languid flow of uncomfortable, peevish silence. "Let them wonder," she whispered again. "But they had better keep their distance."

When Rosie and Lily left the room, Mrs. Washington did her best to gently address the walking hornets' nest that stood beside her without disturbing its venomous interior.

"Something happen today in school that upset you, child?" she said so that only Jasmine could hear.

For all her care, she might as well have pounded the hornets' nest with a baseball bat. A sinister humming began in Jasmine's breast until the frantic occupants could no longer be contained. A thousand angry words burst from her mouth, each with a stinger dripping with poison, each designed to inflict the same pain that Jasmine was feeling so deeply.

"Nothing happened in school today, Momma, that doesn't happen every day of our lives." Each word had been honed to a razor edge and was delivered with careless disregard for the hearer. "I woke up this morning in the same shack after sleeping with the same roaches and rats. I brushed my teeth in the same yellow water and ate whatever was left from supper instead of having a real breakfast. I rode the bus 'cause we got no car, watched the other girls inspect my old dress, them rememberin' that I wore the same one last year, noticin' the hem that's been let out twice, countin' the places where holes have been patched. I can tell what they're thinkin', Momma, and I can guess what they're sayin'."

Jasmine wasn't finished. "I looked out the window on the bus ride home and saw the same White Folks houses and White Folks cars and White Folks antennas for their White Folks television programs. You know what I'm talkin' about, Momma, 'cause they let you in their houses jes so long as you don't touch anything except their ironing and their dirty laundry and their dirty dishes. But we don't belong in those houses, Momma, and we never will."

"And then I have to listen to that crazy Pastor Noah tell me about how much God loves me. Is he blind? Is he stupid? And does he think that I'm so stupid as to believe that *this*," Jasmine waved her hands around the kitchen to remind her mother of the countless examples of poverty and want within her sight, "is how God shows He loves me?"

"If God wants to show me that He love me, I'll be happy to see some clean water comin' out of those pipes over there, and I'll be happy to spread a table cloth and put some hamburgers on this old table, and I'll be happy to wear a nice dress, even if it looks like Betsy McCall's leftovers."

Jasmine drew in a breath and fought back the tears as she looked at her mother. She saw the exhaustion in her mother's eyes and noticed the slump of her tired shoulders. "And if God wants to show us that He loves us, I'll be happy to hear that you don't have to work your fingers to the bone, Momma, just to put bologna on the table. I'd be happy to see *you* in a new dress just once, or drivin' your own car, or going to the movies on a Friday night with your old friends. Oh, Momma."

Jasmine bent over in a flood of tears, the hornets' nest finally emptied of its verbal pests. Mrs. Washington moved to her side and placed her arm around her daughter's shoulders. But Jasmine was not to be comforted. She flung her mother's arm from her and flew out the back door, letting the screen door slam again in testimony to her angry defiance.

Mrs. Washington watched her daughter run into the creek bed behind their house and disappear into the foliage. "Child, child," she said, "what's it gonna take to make you see?" She scraped some crumbling paint from the doorpost with her fingernail. "This is not the real world, child; it's only a rehearsal. Curtain don't go up on the real show for some time now."

Mrs. Washington whispered a short, desperate prayer for her daughter as she watched the light fade on Lanana Creek. And even as she did, another was whispering a similar prayer miles away.

"Lord, you make lame men walk, dumb men talk, blind men see, dead men breathe the breath of life again." Noah and Esther held hands as he lifted his young friend to the place of mercy. "So I know you can do this one little thing for me – help her to see, Lord. Help her to see beyond the visible. You tore the veil once before; do it again, Lord, and let young Jasmine walk into your presence. It's a miracle we need, Lord; that's why we brought her to you. Amen."

Lanana Creek could be a raging torrent after an East Texas thunderstorm, but on this particular evening, after weeks of dry weather, the creek bed was only a rocky path interrupted here and there by a pool of stagnant water.

Jasmine walked with her eyes on the path, balancing on stones and doing her best to keep mud from her only pair of shoes. There was the noise of living coming from the houses that lined the creek, but the canopy of trees and vines that covered the creek softened dramatic voices, clattering pans, slamming doors, and crooning radios so that Jasmine walked in a welcomed world of soft, cool, silence. And in this private, otherwise silent world, her thoughts freely spilled forth.

Who's going to look after Jasmine and her family? Not her good-for-nothing daddy! He's gone for good and they're all better off for it. Can her momma work hard enough to make a difference? Can't happen; she works as hard as a body can and still can't do more than just keep the family's heads above water. Maybe Jasmine will grow up and get a good job. Won't happen; good jobs are for White Folks and college is for White Folks and that means that her folks will just get older and older but never live in any other place and never eat anything other than bologna and cornbread.

The morose monologue continued as Jasmine wound her way along the creek bottom. Jasmine came to the edge of her neighborhood but continued to walk. Ten, fifteen, twenty minutes she walked into, what was for her, unexplored territory.

The sun was fading, the diminished light growing ever fainter when Jasmine caught the first glimpse of orange. What she initially imagined to be a discarded candy wrapper turned out instead to be a single monarch butterfly. In a creek bottom filled with broken bottles, discarded cans, junked cars, and all other sorts of trash, the appearance of this singularly beautiful work of art was a most welcomed contrast. Jasmine stopped and watched the delicate creature drinking from a wet rock, slowly opening and closing its dappled wings as it did.

Suddenly Jasmine was aware of a faint sound, one that she had never heard before, though "sound" is far too harsh a word to describe what she heard. It was as if the air around her was moving on her ears from the gentlest of nudges, from the most subtle of motions.

As Jasmine lifted her eyes from the single butterfly to the canopy of vegetation that surrounded her, her heart almost stopped with what she saw. On every leaf, on every twig, on every branch, on every trunk of every tree, on every twist of every vine, on every discarded can and broken bottle and junked car, on every square inch of surface area that presented itself, there was a glorious monarch butterfly!

And each, in slow measured time, was moving its wings open and closed, open and closed. While the sound of one butterfly opening its wings would be completely indiscernible to the human ear, the sound of a hundred, a thousand, a hundred thousand opening their wings in concert produced the slightest, softest, and most pleasant of sounds.

Jasmine, who realized that she had stopped breathing altogether in the presence of such gentle beauty, took a deep breath of amazement. When she did, the sound of her breathing stirred dozens of the butterflies from their roosts. And when they settled again, they settled not on a twig or leaf or discarded can, but on Jasmine. Jasmine, who had walked into a living work of art, became part of the canvas.

At first, it was a dozen or so on her arms and her dress; then scores on her arms and legs and hair, and then dozens and dozens covering her completely from her shoes to the bow in her hair.

Many people would have been nervous by the closeness and familiarity of so many insects; many would have run screaming at such a visitation. But Jasmine welcomed each visitor as it came, and she became more and more amazed with each additional petal of orange that lit upon her. Each movement of antennae or proboscis or wing was a gentle tickling that caused Jasmine to smile broadly, then giggle softly, then laugh out loud. Who would believe her story?

And then, in a heartbeat, Jasmine's moment of amusement and amazement was transformed into a moment of profundity. She stared again at the details of the creek bottom – the broken bottles, the discarded cans, and the junked cars were all still there. So were the slime-covered rocks and the soggy candy wrappers. But each had been covered by flakes of orange snow so that what was once ugly and offensive was no longer visible; the ugliness had been replaced by a covering of beauty, had been transformed into beauty itself.

And for Jasmine, the walk that had started out in angry accusation and fretful confusion was metamorphosed into calm insight and peaceful acceptance. No one other than her had seen this sight. No one other than her had experienced the mantle of beauty that now adorned her. No one other than her. In an instant, Jasmine knew this moment, this display of transformation and beauty and grace, was for her, for her and her alone!

A hundred preachers offering a thousand sermons, each with the same theme – "God Loves and Cares for You" – would not have taught that lesson to Jasmine as clearly as her butterfly moment in Lanana Creek. It wasn't even hard for her to admit now – Pastor Noah was right, her mother was right, the old Gospel songs were right. God loved her and was fully capable of transforming the ugliness in her life into beauty.

An old man and his wife had prayed, a worrying mother had prayed, a young girl had run into the evening, and the inexplicable had happened. The migration of hundreds of millions of monarch butterflies had halted for the night on the banks of Lanana Creek in Nacogdoches, Texas, and the young girl was forever changed by their visit.

Mrs. Washington was finishing up the dishes. She knew as she looked out the window that it would soon be dark enough to start worrying and searching for Jasmine. But even as she considered the possibility, the form of her oldest daughter climbed out of the creek bed.

Mrs. Washington debated about what to say and how strongly to say it to Jasmine. Would there be more anger, more hurtful words, a long and uncomfortable evening? She swung the screen door open for Jasmine to come in and saw to her great relief that Jasmine's face had been transformed from strained anger into tearful vulnerability.

"Oh, Momma," was all Jasmine could say before she melted into her mother's arms. Mrs. Washington held her trembling, sobbing daughter and stroked her hair as wave after wave of emotion swept over her.

When the storm had passed and apologies had been offered and accepted, Mrs. Washington turned off the kitchen light and the two friends began to get ready for bed.

The Washington household settled down for another night. Pastor Noah and Esther read Scripture and prayed before bed. The rats and roaches on Lanana Street felt the safety of darkness and began to stir once again, and a single monarch butterfly lit on the Washington's back screen and stayed there until morning.

OCTOBER

THE BIRD IN THE HEDGE

Kyle Dexter's body may have been located on this particular October afternoon on Park Street in Nacogdoches, Texas, but his mind was flitting from one exotic location to another. One moment he was in the Pacific Ocean feeling the exhilaration of a Nantucket sleigh ride, and the next he was in darkest Equatorial Africa dodging razor-sharp spears. In one breath, he was hurtling through time to discover what life was like in 20,000 A.D. while in the next he was descending to the very center of the earth.

Kyle turned the *Classics Illustrated* comic over and looked again at its shiny cover – a huge wooden horse towering over the city walls of Troy. *The Iliad* was Ricky's comic, but he and Kyle had an unspoken understanding about sharing and taking care of each other's comics. And because of that, Kyle had to get Ricky's permission to cut out the coupon on the back. The missing coupon on the back was the source of Kyle's daydreams.

At least two weeks before, Kyle had realized that he had saved enough of his allowance to order six *Classics Illustrated* comics. But with over 150 titles listed on the back, choosing only six was a hair-pulling task that gobbled up an entire Saturday afternoon.

On the back of every *Classics Illustrated* comic was this enticement: "Make your selection from these thrilling, exciting, romantic adventure stories. They're only 25 cents postpaid." Kyle had six quarters, and that meant six life-changing journeys into the greatest adventures the world had ever known!

But which six? Many he eliminated in the first round. Titles like *The Crisis*, *The Downfall*, *The Spy* and *The Pilot* ignited no spark in Kyle's imagination. Others like *Buffalo Bill*, *Kit Carson*, and *Daniel Boone* were familiar names but hardly worthy of a 25 cent investment.

Kyle wanted adventure, nail-biting, stomach-turning, heart-racing adventure. Finally, after perusing the entire list four times and labeling each title with one, two, three, or four stars, Kyle made his selection from the four-star finalists: *Moby Dick*, *King Solomon's Mines*, *The Time Machine*, *A Journey to the Center of the Earth*, *The War of the Worlds*, and *Frankenstein*.

He felt guilty not choosing *The Jungle Book*, and it was almost like leaving a loved one behind when he crossed off *Mysterious Island*, but there would be other quarters in the days to come, and Kyle was determined to one day bring all those literary beauties into his comic harem.

The instructions at the bottom of the page said, "Mail coupon below or a facsimile." In too much of a hurry to discover what a facsimile was and doubting seriously if one would actually fit in an envelope, Kyle opted to cut the coupon (with Ricky's permission) and mail it to the far-off and very impressive address: Gilberton Co., Inc. Dept. S. 101 Fifth Avenue, New York, 3, N.Y.

After circling his choices on the coupon and carefully printing his name and address, Kyle faced with this intimidating wording: "Herewith is _____$ for _____ issues of *Classics Illustrated* as circled below." Kyle had watched enough television to know that anything that began with "herewith" was a one-way ticket into serious legal terrain. People were most likely sent to prison on a regular basis for improperly "herewith-ing." In fact, Kyle further imagined, there was probably an entire division of the FBI that dealt solely with "herewith violations."

And so, with much care and trepidation, Kyle filled in the blanks, taped the six quarters to the back of the coupon, and dropped it into an envelope with a thud. It soon became apparent that writing the address on the envelope was a task he should have completed *before* it was sealed tight with quarters inside. Every time the pen hit a quarter, a letter or number underwent a most unusual transformation so that when he was finished, it looked like a right-handed kindergartener had written the address with his left hand.

But a potential postal calamity was averted when Kyle asked his mother for a stamp. Mrs. Dexter, seeing the hieroglyphic nature of the address and feeling the ponderous weight of the contents, made some strategic changes. She replaced four of the quarters with a much lighter dollar bill, recopied the address in a neat, adult hand, affixed a 4-cent stamp, and handed the finished product back to Kyle.

Every great adventure begins with a first step, and the first step for this particular literary adventure was to walk the letter to the mailbox on the corner of Logansport and Park Street. As Kyle allowed the mail drawer to swing closed, butterflies began to stir in the pit of his stomach. The fuse had been lit, the starting pistol had sounded, the topgallant had been unfurled, and adventure would soon be delivered to his front steps.

As the days passed, Kyle refused to allow himself to contemplate where his letter might be or when the magical package might be delivered. In fact, he actively pretended that he had spent the six quarters on something else. That way, when the package arrived, he would not only be delighted but surprised as well.

But it was now two weeks since the letter had been mailed, and Kyle could pretend no longer. He had pictured in his mind's eye what must have already happened at that cryptic New York, 3, N.Y., address. An old, gray-haired man (most likely a retired literature professor from an Ivy League college) had picked up Kyle's letter out of the daily mail delivery. He had slipped a letter opener across the edge and withdrawn the contents, tossed the money into a cigar box on his desk, and leaned back in his chair to examine the order form.

He had tilted his head so that his bifocals focused on the pertinent information. "Kyle Dexter," he mumbled beneath his breath, and then he noticed the list of carefully selected literary gems.

With each choice, he gave a small nod. Halfway through the list, a slight smile showed just below his gray mustache. Upon completing the list, he whispered something like, "A boy after my own heart." Then he swiveled his desk chair so that he faced a wall of shelving filled with comic books, pigeonholes ten high and fifteen across. With easy familiarity, he reached for Kyle's six selections, rolled them in brown paper, sealed the package with glue, affixed the address that Kyle himself had filled out, and dropped the package in a box labeled "Outgoing Mail."

That, Kyle was certain, had already happened, and that meant that any day now, when Mrs. Dexter checked the mail, she would call out, "Kyle, something came for you." And so Kyle waited in sweet anticipation on his bed that bright Saturday morning, hoping that this would be the day his mother announced that Christmas had come early.

But instead of his mother's voice, it was Ricky's that jarred him from his daydream. "Kyle, I need your help! Hurry!"

Kyle felt immediately honored to be needed by his older brother and so followed Ricky in a sprint to the backyard. They ran to a large thick hedge where Ricky's friend, George, was standing with his BB gun. Ricky's gun lay on the ground at George's feet.

"I shot a robin," Ricky said, "but I don't think he's dead. George saw him moving inside the hedge, but we can't get in there. We need you to go in and finish him off."

With those words, Ricky cocked his BB gun and handed it to his younger brother. Kyle, who had never shot a living thing other than roaches, must have shown his reluctance. "He's going to suffer if you don't finish him off," Ricky said.

"You'll be putting him out of his misery," George added.

Kyle's choice was clear – do this thing and the bird's suffering would end; refuse, and the bird's misery would be on his head.

Kyle took the gun, got on his hands and knees, and crawled into the thick hedge. Once inside, it was like being in a world all its own. The bright midday sunlight was filtered through a million leafy shades so that the verdant cave was in perpetual dusk. It would have been a magical place to play and pretend if not for the sordid circumstances that pulled him in on that day.

When Kyle's eyes adjusted to the low light, he noticed that he could stand and move about almost unencumbered. "I don't think he's in here," he shouted and hoped at the same time.

"He's got to be there; look close to the middle." The thick hedge muffled the noises from outside; Ricky seemed to be speaking from a far off place. Kyle searched the ground until he saw what he was hoping he would not see. A large male robin lay on his back with his wings awkwardly outstretched. The rust color of his chest was stained by a bright, unnatural red.

Kyle moved closer and the wings began to flap, but the bird only moved a few inches on the ground. "He's here," Kyle said and stood over the bird.

"Finish him off," Ricky cried from that distant place. It was, after all, the only choice he had. He couldn't let the bird lie there and suffer. It was the only thing to do.

Kyle lowered the cold barrel of the rifle to the bird's head. As he did, the robin began pecking at the barrel, trying to bite it or discourage it or make it go away.

Kyle pulled the barrel back a couple of inches and the robin stopped fighting. As he prepared to pull the trigger, the bird turned his focus from the gun and cocked his head so that he focused his gaze on Kyle instead. The bird was looking at Kyle when he pulled the trigger. The spring was released, the metal sphere was spit from the end of the barrel, and the bird lay dead.

"Did you get him?" the boys asked together. Kyle had never been so close to a wild bird before, and he thought he had never seen anything more beautiful and more heartbreaking. He whispered so that Ricky and George couldn't hear him, "I'm sorry."

At that moment the enormity of what he had done crashed down upon him. Kyle could think of nothing more urgent than escaping that scene of iniquity and death. Instead of going to his hands and knees, he simply tore his way through the hedge. In response, the hedge tore back, leaving Kyle's shirt ripped and his arms and face scratched and bleeding. But that meant nothing to Kyle.

There were already tears in his eyes when George and Ricky saw him, but he didn't care what they saw or what they thought or what they said. He threw the BB gun on the ground and ran sobbing across the yard and through the back screen door.

On his bed with the door closed and a pillow pulled over his head, Kyle wailed as he never had before, as if the Fall of Man had happened all over again. The picture of the dying bird was before him, how it had looked at him before he shot it, how it had done nothing, nothing to deserve the fate it received. And Kyle's heart broke, and he mourned for the loss of the innocent bird and he mourned for the loss of the innocence in his own life.

He had taken a step from which there was no retreat. Kyle had become soiled and dirty and guilty in one instant of time, and he felt as if nothing could wash him clean again.

Kyle moved the comic book on which he was lying, and he remembered the pleasant daydream from just ten minutes before. But the act in the hedge had changed everything. He realized that if his mother had called out that very moment that something had come for him in the mail, he would not have moved from his bed or ceased his sobbing.

In the killing of the bird, Kyle had become a different person, a broken person, a person who didn't smile as often or as easily. His soul had experienced a seismic shift of sorts and all had changed in Kyle's perspective – beauty, significance, goodness, happiness, peace of mind.

In the days that followed, Mrs. Dexter noticed a quieter, more somber Kyle around the house. And when he walked outside, he had the uneasy feeling that all the birds in the trees were watching him, not as they used to watch him, with curiosity and amusement, but with a new sense of caution and with a subtle look of accusation.

Others that knew Kyle noticed the change as well. As one of his Sunday School teachers observed, "It's as if the boy has experienced a death in the family." And she was absolutely correct, but she could never have imagined that the family member Kyle was silently mourning was himself.

LUDIE

A cold October breeze was blowing through the cracks in the frame house on Lanana Street. Ludie Washington pulled a quilt around her as she shuffled the stack of bills piled on the table before her. She shivered from the cold, and she shivered from the prospect of what lay before her and her family.

In the world of financial matters, things were always touch-and-go for Ludie Washington. Working five days a week in other people's homes provided just enough to keep her girls from starving and going naked, but very little more than that. Torn jeans or a ripped coat were inconveniences in most homes, but they were outright tragedies in the Washington household.

With every penny precious, the news of Mrs. Boatwright's death was almost more than Ludie could bear. Dovie Boatwright was Ludie's Tuesday and Thursday employer. Ludie had cooked and ironed and cleaned for the old woman for over two years after it became clear that she couldn't do for herself anymore. Her sudden death not only meant the loss of a dear friend, but it also meant the loss of 40% of Ludie's income.

It was a Saturday morning and Ludie was sitting quietly at the dinner table, contemplating how in the world she was going to make it with only three days of work each week and the same monthly pile of bills. She knew it was wrong to be fretting and worrying and feeling sorry for herself. Rocking back and forth, she let out a low, "Laud, Laud," just as her oldest daughter walked by.

"Mama, what's the matter?"

Wiping away a tear, she realized she might as well come clean with the bad news. "We're going to have some rough times ahead, Sweetheart; Miss Dovie's passing means I only work for Miss Patterson now. Things are gonna be tight; I'm sorry, child, but things are gonna be tight."

With those words, the brave woman began to weep. She had worked so hard to provide for her babies; she had never asked for anything for herself. It just didn't seem fair that God would jerk the rug from beneath her feet when she had nothing but a hard, cold floor to land on.

Her daughter wrapped her arms around her mother's shoulders and the two of them rocked back and forth together, their tears commingling into an unspoken prayer for help.

"Don't worry, Mama. You need to remember what you tell us over and over, that His eye is on the sparrow and I know He watches me."

Ludie wiped her tears, a bit embarrassed that her daughter was encouraging her instead of the other way around, but also proud of the fact, proud of the way she had learned and grown.

"You're right," she said. "We're gonna be fine; His eye is on the sparrow, so He's certainly gonna look after my babies and me."

In Kyle's estimation, it didn't take much to be an award-winning Sunday School student at First Christian Church. Basically, all you had to do was show up. Every year on Graduation Sunday, students were given Sunday School certificates that bore testimony to the fact that they had graduated from one class and had been promoted to the next. Each was signed by the appropriate Sunday School teacher and co-signed by Pastor Dexter. The two signatures made the document legally official, in case the issue was ever challenged in open court.

And you didn't even have to behave! Kyle knew this was true as year after year he watched cut-ups and scoundrels promoted along with the more subdued, well-behaved students.

Silver stars were given out every week for attendance, and an additional gold star was given for every month of perfect attendance. And Kyle never missed a Sunday! Of course, living next door to the church and having the pastor as his father didn't hurt.

Sunday School consisted of showing up, taking an offering, listening to a Bible story, and coloring a denominational Sunday School handout. That is until you reached the fourth grade!

There was a quantum leap in requisite cerebral activity from third grade Sunday School to fourth grade Sunday School and it was all because of the fourth grade teacher, Miss Letha Moorer.

Miss Moorer was in her 60's, had been teaching fourth graders for dozens of years, and had it down to a science. Her passion was for Scripture memory, a passion that would have been oppressive and legalistic if it were not for her additional passions for God and His little lambs.

The first day in the class was quite a shock for all those third grade graduates who were looking for the crayons and a coloring sheet. "This year," she said as her eyes twinkled above her reading glasses, "we are going to memorize God's Word."

Miss Moorer sat with her hands folded on the table in front of her and her Bible open to an appropriate passage. On her face was the expectant smile of a daring explorer, a seasoned guide who was poised to lead her naïve charges into a hitherto unexplored world of beauty and truth. And her head was crowned with waves of flaming red hair, a fitting attribute for one whose heart was so on fire for God and His Word.

Since the school year began, her class had memorized The Lord's Prayer, The Good Confession, The 23rd Psalm, and had started on The Beatitudes. But everyone knew the big challenge was coming after Christmas when they would be required to memorize The Love Chapter, the entirety of 1st Corinthians 13! Gold stars were earned in fourth grade Sunday School!

The bell sounded to end the Sunday School hour; a dozen doors flew open and a well-dressed wave of young people poured down the stairs to meet their parents for church, except for Kyle and Donna and Ricky. Their dad, of course, sat on the platform up front. And their mom sat with the choir for the entire worship service. The Dexter kids were on their own for the worship hour.

Donna and Ricky typically sat with friends and their families. Kyle took another tack.

In looking around for someone to sit with, Kyle noticed that Mrs. Patterson was sitting by herself. He slid on the pew beside her and asked, "Can I sit with you?" Even though she had been an elementary teacher for over 20 years, she refused to correct his word choice. Instead, she smiled like it was Christmas morning and opened her arms in welcome.

Observers may have assumed that it was Kyle's tender heart that directed him to this woman who would otherwise be sitting alone. While Kyle's heart was, on occasion, bent toward acts of compassion, there were, on this particular morning, other reasons for his choice.

The first of which was that Mrs. Patterson smelled like a flower. The gardenia-scented fragrance that announced her coming and lingered after her passing attracted Kyle like a bee to a blossom. How could you sit anywhere else when every breath beside Mrs. Patterson was a visit to a scented garden?

But her delicious fragrance came in a distant second to the primary reason he sat with her that morning. Since it was a chilly morning, Mrs. Patterson had worn her fox stole, and it was a virtual magnet for a fourth grade boy.

In the first place, the foxes were still there! There were two of them, one biting onto the tail of his former companion to make a wrap long enough to cover a woman's shoulders. And their ears and noses and marble eyes and actual teeth were all begging to be touched and explored by nine-year-old naturalists everywhere. And Mrs. Patterson was more than willing to cooperate.

And while the foxes' faces were a treat to explore, the fox fur was like heaven to touch. The sometimes tiresome experience of listening to his father's sermon flew by in an instant as Kyle petted and stroked the fox stole nonstop. He was almost sorry to hear his father say the solemn "Amen" that indicated the sermon was over – almost.

In choosing Mrs. Patterson for a seating companion, Kyle had no way of knowing that the choice would start a string of events and relationships that would change his family forever.

As the congregation milled around and chatted, Mrs. Dexter joined Kyle and Mrs. Patterson. The two ladies talked for a moment until the conversation turned to Mrs. Dexter's desire to find someone to help with her ironing for a couple of days each week. Kyle was walking away to be with friends when he heard Mrs. Patterson say, "If she's available, I could bring her over to meet you this very afternoon."

Sunday lunch was over and the Dexter children had cleared the table, swept the floor, and washed the dishes. Three jobs, three kids. It was a perfect arrangement with responsibilities shifting every week.

Kyle was lying on the living room couch listing to a Kingston Trio record when the phone rang. Mrs. Dexter answered the phone, spoke for a moment, and told Kyle to run upstairs to get Donna. Ricky was already at his friend George's house or he would have been summoned, too.

"Mrs. Patterson is bringing over a lady who is going to help us out on Tuesdays and Thursdays. Her name is Ludie Washington. You may call her Ludie."

"Can we just wait upstairs while y'all talk?" Kyle asked. Since kids are often in the way and since adults often like to talk about adult stuff, Kyle thought his suggestion was an especially brilliant one.

"Absolutely not," Mrs. Dexter replied, straightening up the living room in preparation for the visitors. "You'll be seeing Ludie before you go to school twice a week, so you need to get to know her."

A moment later Mrs. Patterson's car pulled into the Dexter driveway. There was the sound of car doors opening and closing, and then the doorbell rang.

Kyle and Donna sat on the couch and heard introductions made and greetings exchanged. Mrs. Dexter and Ludie walked into the living room leaving Mrs. Patterson chatting with Ludie's children in the hall. When Kyle saw Ludie for the first time, he thought he had never before seen such a warm and welcoming person. Her skin was the blackest he had ever seen, her teeth were the whitest, and her eyes the most expressive.

With dancing eyes, she laughed out the words, "Ooooooh, this must be Kyle!" And then she laughed some more. Kyle had the feeling that he had been a topic of conversation between Ludie and Mrs. Patterson. He wondered what Mrs. Patterson had told her that elicited such an enthusiastic "Oooooooh."

Kyle smiled and shook Ludie's strong hand. Then Mrs. Dexter introduced her to Donna. Kyle looked at Donna to see if she was as taken by Ludie as he was, but Donna's eyes and expression conveyed fear, not delight.

When Kyle looked back at Ludie, he saw the reason. Standing just behind Ludie, with eyes as wide with surprise as their own, was Ludie's oldest daughter, Jasmine, the girl who had taken their library books and so thoroughly frightened them during the last week of summer.

Donna managed to recover enough to greet Ludie, but without her usual smile and bubbly personality. Then, as if things were not uncomfortable enough, Mrs. Dexter said, "Donna, why don't you and Kyle show Jasmine your rooms while Ludie and I talk about next week." Mrs. Patterson was on the couch with Rosie sitting beside her and Lily in her lap.

Without a word, Donna and Kyle led the way up the stairs with Jasmine reluctantly following behind them. In Donna's room, they each stood like the points of a triangle, each silently staring at the other two.

It was at that most uncomfortable moment that Jocko, Donna's parakeet, broke the silence. "Put your britches on; put your britches on," it said. Jasmine, who had never heard a bird speak and who had never imagined that one could tell you to put your britches on, was overwhelmed with amazement. In spite of her guilt over her past actions, she simply had to ask the question.

"Did that bird just talk?"

Donna and Kyle had heard Jocko talk for years and occasionally forgot how unusual it was. "Yes," Donna answered, then added, "he talks all the time."

Jasmine, still not believing what she had heard, asked again, "But did he just say, 'Put your britches on'?"

Donna, with a chance to talk, did not let the opportunity slip by.

"His cage used to be downstairs, and every morning Ricky and Kyle would come downstairs in their underwear and my mom would say, 'Put your britches on.' One day, after she had said it for a long time, Jocko started saying it too. Watch."

Donna went to the cage and said in her best imitation bird voice, "Put your britches on; put your britches on."

Jocko replied on cue, "Put your britches on; put your britches on," and the three laughed together.

Kyle, not wanting to be left out and wanting desperately to change the subject away from him in his underwear, said, "Watch this."

He stood before Jocko's cage and began to bob his head up and down. Jocko became his mirror reflection and bobbed his head in unison with Kyle. The three laughed again.

Kyle resumed his place and the three points of the triangle quietly considered the other two once more. It was Jasmine who finally mentioned the topic that was on every mind.

"Are you gonna tell?" It was asked quietly and with great concern. There was no threatening nature to the words. "About the time with the books last summer?" The angry girl of Lanana Street was gone; she had been replaced by a frightened girl on Park Street.

Donna had no way of knowing that Jasmine asked the question because she was afraid of being punished by her mother. But more than that, Jasmine was terribly afraid that her mother would lose the position in the Dexter household because of what her daughter had done. And even more than that, she was brokenhearted and ashamed over how she had treated the two children who stood before her.

Donna had no way of knowing Jasmine's motives, no way of knowing beyond the ability of one soul to read the depths of another. And Donna read contrition and fear and humility in Jasmine's question, and she answered in kind.

"I don't even remember that ol' morning, do you, Kyle?" Kyle, who had been watching the two interact, was suddenly drawn into the mix. "Do you remember that time, Kyle?"

Kyle followed Donna's lead as he had so many times before, and this time, with a touch of flair all his own. "Ever since I started fourth grade, all I can think about is long division and cursive writin'. I can't remember any days before that."

Jasmine's pained look became a soft smile. Three children had resolved an issue that might have caused feuds or riots or wars if it had been turned over to the care of adults. But not knowing the sophisticated ways of grown-ups, they simply forgave and went on.

Jasmine's eyes explored Donna's room. "Is that an Easy-Bake Oven?" Donna had gotten it two Christmases before.

"Yeah," Kyle answered, "but we ate all the cakes and cookies the first week we had it."

"One of my friends had one," Jasmine added, "and she did the same thing."

As she continued to look around the room, her eyes fell on Donna's open closet. The variety and quantity of dresses, skirts, blouses, sweaters, and coats seemed to Jasmine like the racks of Beall Brothers department store downtown.

"Are all those dresses yours?"

"Yeah," Donna said, but not wanting to seem too proud, she added, "but a lot of them don't fit me anymore."

Jasmine, who had a school dress and a church dress, couldn't believe the choices Donna had each morning when she dressed for school. Her mouth hung open in disbelief – she was in the presence of a living, breathing Betsy McCall!

"Girls! Kyle!" It was Mrs. Dexter from downstairs. "Ludie's leaving now." The three scurried down the stairs. Mrs. Patterson and the Washington family said their goodbyes and the Dexter household was quiet and peaceful again.

"Well, what do you think of Ludie?" Mrs. Dexter asked.

"I like her a lot," Kyle answered.

"Me, too," added Donna.

"And what do you think of Jasmine?"

"Who's Jasmine?" Donna asked.

Mrs. Dexter laughed. "That's the name of the girl you spent the last 15 minutes with. How is it you spent 15 minutes together and didn't even learn each other's names? What did you kids talk about anyway?"

Donna looked at Kyle. "Oh, other stuff," she said. "Come on, Kyle. Let's see if we can find something to cook in the Easy-Bake Oven."

GRACE NOTES

It was a Saturday afternoon and life should have been slow and sweet for Kyle, highlighted by some casual play, a western movie on television, or a leisurely perusal through his personal stash of comic books. But good things were not to be.

Kyle was putting on a starched shirt and doing his best to keep the stiff collar from resting on his neck. "Stop that," his mother said, watching his pained contortions. "You look like a turtle peeking out of his shell."

His mom had told him multiple times that no one had ever died from a starched shirt, but Kyle was not persuaded. Furthermore, he was not convinced that mercifully dying from starch poisoning could be any worse than the torture of feeling a sticky collar on his tender neck for hours at a time. And Kyle knew that he would be spending hours in that starched shirt on this particular Saturday afternoon.

He tried not to move as he sat in the back seat of the Dexter's '58 Chevy, Ricky and Donna on either side. If he kept perfectly still and poked his head forward just a bit, the starched collar was temporarily rendered harmless.

Even though Kyle had to wear a scratchy shirt, he realized that Ricky and Donna had it far worse than he did. They were going to have to play the piano in front of dozens of strangers in a matter of minutes and possibly make such utter fools of themselves that the entire Dexter family might be forced to leave town under the cover of darkness. With that picture in mind, the thought of wearing a starched shirt didn't seem quite so bad.

Mamie Meadows was a widow woman who loved music and loved children. She gave piano lessons in her home on most afternoons in order to supplement her meager resources but also, and more importantly, to keep the specters of aging and loneliness at bay.

There would be 15 of her beloved pupils playing their recital pieces that afternoon, witnessed by siblings, parents, and grandparents. Mrs. Meadows' living room was filled to capacity with rows of folding chairs, each with Oakley-Metcalf Funeral Home stenciled on the back. Kyle felt the choice of chairs was highly appropriate as he settled in to watch the musical wake unfold.

Mrs. Meadows smiled and welcomed the excited group to her home and spoke a moment about the virtue of loving music. She read a few lines from Shakespeare's *Merchant of Venice* to emphasize her point. Kyle couldn't understand most of it, but he understood enough to conclude that if he didn't come to love music, he would most likely end up dead or in prison.

The procession of artists began, the youngest first. After the first two or three performers, Kyle made an observation that quickly turned into a game. As soon as each student was applauded and returning to their seat, Kyle closed his eyes until the next student was playing. Then he would look around the room and try to determine which parents went with that particular student.

It was a cinch! All he had to do was look for the couple with goofy smiles on their faces, the ones visibly leaning forward in their chairs out of a strange combination of robust pride and intense dread.

One girl about his age had memorized her recital piece. She got to a particular place in the song and stopped. She started over and came to a dead stop at exactly the same place. The third time she played it much faster, hoping that speed would allow her to burst through the mental roadblock and finish the song. It only brought her to the embarrassing place more quickly.

The crowd was visibly uncomfortable, everyone aching for the young girl to succeed. The ordeal seemed to drag on forever! Finally, on what felt like the 10th try, Mrs. Meadows whispered something to her at the appropriate place and she finished the song with flair.

As the audience applauded and the young girl took her seat, her grandmother could be heard to say in a rather accusatory voice, "No wonder she had trouble; they gave her such a long piece!"

Donna played a song about a bumblebee that ended with her saying "Ouch" as she played the final note. Her performance got a good laugh and a solid round of applause.

Ricky played a piece called "The Little Indian." With one hand he struck two keys over and over to simulate the sound of a beating drum. With the other hand, he played the melody. Kyle thought it was a very good performance as did the audience.

When Ricky was finished, Mrs. Meadows rose and announced that she had one more student who was going to play. When the final student got to her feet, Kyle realized that something different was about to happen.

He had been watching this young lady on and off throughout the recital. She was as tall as Kyle's mother, but Kyle couldn't tell if she was 15 or 30. She wore a simple blue dress, had a most unassuming haircut, and a lower jaw that seemed to protrude a bit too much.

Kyle had seen her waving her hand like an orchestra conductor while the recital was going on. And several times she had turned around and stared at members of the audience in a most uninhibited manner.

As she approached the piano, Kyle tapped his mother on the knee to signal that he had a question. Mrs. Dexter kept her eyes to the front, put her hand on Kyle's, and held it still as if to say, "Not now."

The young lady spread out her music and labored to find the place on the piano where her finger needed to go. And it was only one finger that played.

She hit the first note and waited, and waited, and waited. After a painfully long silence, she finally hit the second note, so long after the first that it was hard to remember what the first note had been. Kyle began to squirm out of discomfort, out of his fear of an approaching disaster. He could picture the humiliating failure that lay ahead, the tears, the shamed artist fleeing from the room. He held his breath and waited for it to come.

A third note came and finally a fourth and a light came on in Kyle's brain. He pulled on his mother's sleeve until her ear was close and he whispered, "I'll bet a thousand dollars I know what the next note is going to be!" The fifth note was struck and Kyle smiled and nodded, as if to say, "I knew it!" Mrs. Dexter smiled back and they both listened.

Even though the individual notes were separated by immense stretches of silence, the melody of the song was becoming clear to all who heard it. It was a hymn they sang at First Christian on occasion, "Be Thou My Vision," and while the young lady played it slowly, she played each note in its appropriate order.

The song finally came to a conclusion and the audience breathed a collective sigh of relief. But the young lady did not move from the piano; instead, she simply scooted as far to the right on the piano bench as she could go. The reason for her movement became clear as Mrs. Meadows took a seat on the bench beside her. And then a musical miracle came to pass.

Once again the young lady struck the first note of the hymn, but instead of an awkward silence following the note, Mrs. Meadows played two chords and the single note was no longer alone but was supported and enhanced and gloriously fleshed out. And then the second note was sounded, no longer asking the audience to remember, if they could, the note that preceded it, but daring them to forget the majestic swell of music that preceded and followed it.

And so the whole hymn was played, a single note by the fledgling student followed by a sweeping display of harmonious support by the master musician. Kyle felt strangely moved as he listened. When he looked at his mom, he saw that she was crying, and he realized that he was on the verge of tears himself.

The song was completed; the master and her student stood together and the enthusiastic crowd did their best to repay the gift they had received with their thunderous applause.

As the students and their families milled around and talked, each with a cup of punch and a plate of cookies, Kyle sat in the most remote of the folding chairs and thought. He was so deep in thought that he neither enjoyed the punch and cookies nor did he chafe at his starchy collar.

Something had happened that afternoon and Kyle knew that it was something very important; he just didn't know what it was. Two people were playing music and he was almost crying about it and he didn't know why.

Kyle realized that, without seeing her approach, his mother was sitting beside him. "What'cha thinking about?" she asked. It was the question that mothers ask of their little ones when they are burdened by profundity and need some help bearing the load.

"I don't know," Kyle replied, realizing that his thoughts were not the type you could put to words. You can talk about not liking what's on your dinner plate, or wishing that a certain girl would like you, or being scared about going to the dentist, but what do you say about this?

Kyle thought for a moment and tried. "Sometimes, when something happens, can it mean something else?" His mom's eyes narrowed in thought and she asked for clarification, "What do you mean, Kyle? What are you thinking?"

Kyle proceeded cautiously, feeling himself on the threshold of some sacred discovery, in the presence of some holy truth. "When the two ladies were playing together, I started feeling like it meant something else. When I listened to them play, I felt like," he whispered the rest, "like I wanted to cry. And I don't even know what made me sad."

Mrs. Dexter smiled. "You weren't sad, Kyle; we cry for lots of reasons and it's not always because we're sad. Sometimes, like today, we cry because something is beautiful, or," and here she whispered, as if it was their secret, "sometimes we cry because something means something else. Don't worry; you'll figure it out."

Instead of driving straight home, Mr. Dexter drove one block over and into the parking lot of Wallace's Dairy Queen. The backseat erupted in cheers. It was a rare occasion when the Dexter household ate anything other than Mrs. Dexter's cooking, but today was a special day and this was a way to celebrate.

"Who wants a hamburger?" Mr. Dexter incited his backseat into cheers once more.

"No tomatoes on mine," said Ricky. "No onions on mine," said Kyle. Donna smiled and added that she would like everything on hers, please. Mr. Dexter walked to the window to place his order.

The smell of hamburgers was in the air, the sun was dipping behind the pine trees, and a cool breeze was blowing through the car's open windows. Kyle laid his weary head back, closed his eyes, and began thinking about the musical miracle he had witnessed that afternoon. Once again, he began to feel that warm, teary grip on his heart.

With his eyes closed, somewhere between a crisply focused reality and a softly indistinct world of dreams, a bank of clouds parted and a ray of light broke through. The clouds that parted were not above the Dairy Queen but were in fact in Kyle's heart and mind. And the ray of light that broke through illuminated and clarified the truth that Kyle had been seeking.

The young lady playing her simple note and the skilled master expanding that note into majestic fullness – it did mean something else, something more after all. Kyle understood.

He, Kyle, was the simple note player! His greatest efforts to make a difference and to do good and to be good were, at best, a single, simple note rightly played. But the note he played would never be enough, even as he became older and wiser; it would never be good enough!

But, and the thought almost took Kyle's breath away, he would not be playing his piece alone. Another would be sitting beside him who could take his simple note and transform it, expand it into an achingly beautiful song.

The burden from the playground, the weight that Kyle had recently placed on his own heart, was being mercifully lifted. He no longer had to figure out this life by himself. He no longer had to be good enough so that everyone would love him. Kyle realized that whatever this life was going to require of him, it could never overwhelm him, it could never be too much. The Master was by his side; it would be all right.

One more image from the afternoon flooded Kyle's inner eye. He saw once again, this time with greater understanding, the master teacher smiling down on her struggling student. The smile did not fade with clumsiness nor did it grow with proficiency. It was the same smile no matter what, and it was the same smile he had seen all afternoon – a smile of parental pride and unwavering love. And Kyle understood: that was how the Master regarded him.

And his tender heart, unable to hold the fullness of such a thought, began to overflow with tears.

"Kyle, what's wrong?" Donna asked. He shook his head and tried to hold back the tears.

"Momma, what's wrong with Kyle?" she asked again. Mrs. Dexter looked back at Kyle; their eyes met and she read his heart, and he kept it open for her to read.

"He's fine," she said, her eyes never leaving Kyle's. "It's just that we learned today that sometimes things are so beautiful and wonderful that it is impossible to explain them with words." She smiled. "So we explain them with tears."

MONSTERS

They had seen it advertised on television all week and had planned for hours their strategy for being in the viewing audience. The announcer had made his voice deeper and had affected his best British accent.

"Halloween is still a week away, but this year, HORROR gets an early start! Join us this Saturday evening at 8:00 for a presentation, with limited commercial interruptions, of Boris Karloff in *Frankenstein*."

As the announcer spoke, a still image of Boris Karloff as Frankenstein's monster drew closer and closer until all Donna and Kyle could see were a pair of shadowy, sunken, inhuman eyes.

They had literally shivered with excitement at the prospect of watching such a classic horror film. Mr. Dexter had spoken of seeing the movie with his mother when it first hit the big screen back in the early 30's. It had not gone well.

Arriving late, the two were forced to find a seat on the front row of Sulphur Springs' Misson Theater, a wide-eyed farm boy of six and his very proper, somewhat rigid mother. The first few minutes of the movie had gone reasonably well, but when the body parts started showing up—hands, eyes, brain—Kyle's grandmother had had enough.

"Well," she said, loud enough so that the entire audience could hear. She plucked her completely engrossed son to his feet by his shirt collar and towed him to the exit. All the way up the aisle, young Donald Dexter savored every frame and every sound until the large cushioned door to the lobby swung shut. At 35, he still had never seen the ending of the movie.

Donna and Kyle had an entire week to make sure that nothing similar happened to them. They began by cleverly planting seeds of ideas in their parents' minds.

Idea # 1: Television does not frighten us.

Monday evening at the dinner table Donna glanced at Kyle and he responded with a quick, almost imperceptible nod.

"Momma, what's the scariest show you've ever seen on television?" Donna asked the question as if it had been randomly floating through the universe until it providentially nested in her brain.

"I guess some of those Science Fiction Theatre episodes we used to watch when we lived in Mason. The one about the man-eating fungus really gave me the willies."

That was Kyle's cue, and he waited just the right length of time before he said, "Really? I don't think that one was scary at all."

Mrs. Dexter was just about to remind Kyle that he slept between her and Mr. Dexter that night, but Donna followed his comment with her own.

"I guess things on television just aren't that scary. I guess it's hard to be frightened by something on so small a screen."

There; it had been said. The seed had been planted by the pair of nefarious schemers. With a little time and the encouragement of good behavior, it could grow into a fully-blossomed conviction!

But one seed was not enough when such a valuable harvest was at stake. And so another seed was planted.

Idea # 2: It is impossible to deny the requests of cute and cooperative children.

Donna and Kyle began to closely resemble children that graced the covers of *The Saturday Evening Post*. They cleared the table without being asked, swept the leaves from the driveway, and kept their school books and shoes out of the living room. Kyle even took a mid-week bath. They were pulling out all the stops.

On Tuesday, Donna asked her mother, "Is there anything I can do to help you this evening?" Mrs. Dexter was delightfully surprised by the offer and gave Donna a big hug.

"Thank you, Sweetheart; but I think I have everything under control tonight."

On Wednesday, it was Kyle's turn at the charade. "Can I help you with anything tonight, Mom?" Kyle waited to receive his smile and hug and was caught off guard when his mother said, "Why yes, I forgot to get the clothes off the line. Would you do that for me, Sweetheart?"

Getting the clothes off the line was one thing, but doing it at night with only the porch light to guide you was a terrifying experience. But Kyle didn't say a word, didn't show an ounce of fear.

Clothespin after clothespin clicked into the canvas bag; garment after garment dropped into the plastic hamper. On more than one occasion, the memory of those Frankenstein eyes seemed to materialize in the dark over the clothesline. Each time, Kyle closed his eyes and stood still until he had the nerve to continue. Finally, the clothes were gathered and a much-shaken Kyle was back in the safety of his lighted living room.

"I think I'll go work on some Math," he said as he walked up to his bedroom.

Wagon Train was on the television, but Kyle had shown absolutely no interest in something so trifling, something that so grievously interfered with a pursuit as worthwhile as homework. He savored the impression that he must have made as he climbed the stairs to his room.

At last, the big night arrived. Mr. and Mrs. Dexter had been in the yard and were about to walk through the front door. Kyle and Donna quickly took their pre-arranged places behind the couch. When the front door closed, they popped up from behind the couch with cherubic smiles and dancing eyes and cried out in unison, "Can we watch *Frankenstein* tonight?"

"*May* we watch *Frankenstein* tonight," their mother corrected. Kyle, not realizing he had been corrected thought, "See, Mom and Dad want to watch it, too!" But Donna submitted to the grammatical reproof and repeated the amended request, "May we watch *Frankenstein* tonight?"

"I don't know, Sweetheart," their mother said, "it's really scary. You probably wouldn't sleep for a week!"

To most kids that answer would have sounded like some form of "no," but to both Kyle and Donna the presence of the phrase "I don't know" meant that they had already won.

That conditional phrase in the Dexter household universally meant, "You're asking for something big, and I'm going to let you have it. But before I say 'yes,' let me act a bit hesitant and throw out a couple of reasons why I should say 'no.' It's what good parents do, so bear with me for a few minutes."

Kyle and Donna played the game. "Please, please; we've been good!"

"Well, they have been being good," Mr. Dexter observed. "I guess it wouldn't hurt just this once."

The cheering and dancing and clapping continued until Mr. Dexter interrupted. "But remember, if there are any problems, this will be the last time! Kyle, are you going to be able to sleep by yourself when this is over?" Ricky was spending the night at George's house and wouldn't be available for emergency monster intervention.

Kyle, laughing at the thought of such childish behavior, promised that there would be no problems as far as he was concerned.

And so the venture was complete. The seeds had been planted and watered and thoroughly fertilized, and they had finally blossomed into this incomparable privilege.

It was 8:00 and the Dexter 15" Zenith was ablaze. Mr. Dexter had spent 5 minutes with the vertical control knob and was finally satisfied when the movie began.

Kyle and Donna huddled together on the couch as the title burst upon the screen. The music was horrifying; even the lettering of the title was frightening. The story hadn't even begun and Kyle and Donna were already terrified.

For the next two hours, image after horrifying image was flashed across that tiny screen. And despite Donna's reasoning, the size of the screen did nothing to minimize the horror the two felt.

"Are you all right?" Mrs. Dexter asked during every commercial break. Donna and Kyle answered in the affirmative, but their racing hearts, their wide eyes, their audible gasps, and the numerous times they covered their eyes with their hands conveyed a different answer.

Finally, mercifully, the movie ended and it was time to go to bed. Donna and Kyle walked up the stairs together. Donna's bedroom was at the top of the stairs; Kyle's was at the end of the hall – the dark, menacing hall!

"Don't close the door until I turn my light on," Kyle pleaded. The wooden floor creaked as he made his way to his darkened room. He reached inside, flipped the light on, and heard Donna say, "Goodnight," as she closed her bedroom door. He was alone!

Kyle noticed that his closet door was ajar. Why hadn't he closed it earlier! Of course, he would have to close it now; it would be foolish to leave that gaping blackness visible through the night, that open doorway into the world of fear and imaginings. Kyle carefully closed the closet door.

The bulb in Kyle's bedside lamp had been burned out for a week. He kicked himself for not replacing it in the benign hours of daylight. He would have to make the trip from the light switch to his bed in complete darkness.

Kyle quickly got on his pajamas and turned down his covers. He cleared the path between the light switch and his bed of random toys and clothes, and he readied himself for the most important run of his young life.

He looked down the darkened hall to where the stairs disappeared around the corner. He could imagine the monster's thumping steps as he made his way up the stairs. First, his sewn-on hand would appear on the banister, and then his stitched-up head with those sinister eyes would peer around the corner. Kyle knew that once his eyes met the monster's eyes, he would be frozen in fear and his fate would be sealed.

Kyle took a deep breath, visualized his path to the bed, and flipped off the light. As darkness enveloped the room, Kyle took his first step toward the bed. What was wrong with his legs? They moved clumsily and felt unnaturally heavy. He felt as if he was running in the city swimming pool, as if his feet were stuck in mud.

Kyle was waiting to feel the monster's hot breath on his neck, expecting the monster's hand to grab him as he moved to his bed, found its edge, hopped in, pulled the covers to his neck and squeezed his eyes tight.

It was here that Kyle's expert knowledge of monsters' strengths and monsters' weaknesses most likely saved his life.

As almost every boy knows, monsters cannot hurt you if you are asleep. This is blatantly obvious from the fact that young boys go to sleep each night, monsters prowl each night, and those same young boys wake up in the morning. If monsters could harm young boys when they slept, Kyle would have noticed the number of boys in his classroom steadily declining as the school year progressed. But the same number of boys that started in Mrs. Hartsfield's class in September still showed up in late October. Kyle's reasoning was ironclad: monsters cannot harm you while you sleep.

But Kyle's knowledge of monsters did not stop with this universally accepted axiom. He also knew that monsters cannot harm you if you *give every appearance of being asleep*, even if you are wide awake. While monsters are thoroughly evil, they are not altogether intelligent and, if a young boy is clever enough, may be fooled into believing that he is asleep.

With such a deception in mind, Kyle relaxed his eyes and steadied his breathing. His covers were to his neck and his hands were under the covers, at his sides.

The novice in all-things-monster might have made the common mistake of pulling the covers completely over his head. While this would temporarily have solved one problem (being seen by the monster), it would have created another problem that could potentially be disastrous.

For unless the night is deep in December and frightfully cold, the head-under-the-cover approach will eventually lead to unbearably hot and stuffy conditions that will force the enshrouded one to withdraw his head from the covers, revealing that he is obviously awake, and therefore subjecting him to monster attacks. All things said, it is best to keep the head above the covers.

As he lay in bed, giving every appearance of being asleep, Kyle was beset with image after image from the movie he had just seen. He could see the monster's jaw set in malevolent determination and he could still hear his low, animalistic growl. There was danger in Kyle's next thought, but he knew he needed to take a quick peek around the room to see if any monsters were visible.

Keeping his breathing steady and one eye perfectly closed, he slowly, slightly lifted one eyelid so he could make a quick survey of his room. Then he saw it! To his horror, he saw the zigzag stitching on the monster's brow brightly glowing across the room. Kyle's heart almost stopped, and he squeezed his eyes shut again.

He had watched the movie in spite of his mother's words of warning. And in doing so, he had invited to his own bedroom the monster who was at that very moment, drawing near.

Kyle contemplated the glowing zigzag, first with a racing heart and then, when he finally realized what it was, with a much calmer spirit.

Mr. Patterson, who went to Kyle's church, worked for Texas Power and Light. He had given Kyle a plastic figure of Ready Kilowatt, the TP&L mascot. Ready had a round light socket for a head, and arms and legs of jagged bolts of electricity. And the arms and legs were of glow-in-the-dark material. That was the glowing zigzag that Kyle had seen in the dark.

Kyle lay still and tried to sleep, but his mind was too full of the monster. It was in that moment, as he lay there on that monster-filled night, that he created a game that would calm and comfort him in that moment and for years to come.

As Kyle reflected on commonly held monster lore, he remembered that monsters cannot see through covers. Only God can see through covers; monsters are able to see only what is left out in the open.

Kyle's hands were under the covers, lying beside him. His fingers were next to his legs and as such, could move ever so slightly without disturbing the covers and alerting ever-vigilant monsters that he was awake.

Each of the hands was in a sort of cave formed by the covers on one side and his leg or the other. And in those caves, his fingers could move without the monster being aware of it.

But in Kyle's mind, these were not simply fingers, they were soldiers of the U. S. Army, and not just any soldiers in the U. S. Army; they were Sgt. Rock and the men of Easy Company!

Kyle had several of their comic books. Sgt. Rock and the devil-may-care men of Easy Company were tough with the enemy and tender with civilians; they could laugh at each other's foibles, and they could cry when someone close to them was lost. But when it came to engaging in battle against the Germans, they were fearless! Whether it was Germans they were facing or monsters, you couldn't ask for braver, truer friends to have at your side than Sgt. Rock and the men of Easy Company.

Kyle carefully moved his fingers beneath the covers. Sgt. Rock and his gallant gang of warriors laughed and talked around the warm fire in the secluded cave. They cleaned their rifles and readied themselves for the next threat to their lives and their liberty.

Beginning on that night, a carefree troop of GI's became Kyle's ever-present friends and protectors. Whenever monsters prowled in Kyle's bedroom (and it was a rare night when they didn't), Sgt. Rock and the men of Easy Company sharpened their bayonets and dared them to draw near. And with such brave men by his side, Kyle slept without fear.

NOVEMBER

PASTOR DEXTER'S STAND

Donald Dexter stepped out of his front door into the Saturday night darkness. It was just after 11:30 as he carefully made his way across the lawn to the church building. The north wind was steady and cold, and it would be stronger and colder before morning. And that was the very reason he was outside on a cold Saturday night.

Living in the parsonage next to the church was wonderfully convenient at times, but it also meant that if something last-minute needed to be done in the church building, well, there was no more logical choice than Pastor Donald Dexter to do it. With a strong cold front scheduled to hit about midnight, Pastor Dexter knew that the sanctuary would be miserably cold if he waited until morning to adjust the heat.

First Christian Church, with its blond bricks and high steeple, was one of the most beautiful and stately churches in Nacogdoches. But like so many built in that era, it used exceptionally high ceilings and open windows to deal with the oppressive heat of the East Texas summers. And when winter came, those same high ceilings meant that the furnace needed to be on all night to keep exposed ankles and knees from shaking during the Sunday morning sermon.

With the thermostat adjusted and the door locked, Pastor Dexter turned up the collar of his well-worn corduroy jacket and headed for home and bed. But before he made it to the front door, a car slowly pulled to the curb and stopped, immediately in front of the church parsonage. The flashing lights of the patrol car that pulled up behind it told the rest of the story.

Pastor Dexter slowed his pace and watched the scene unfold before him. A young police officer stepped from his car and swaggered to the driver's side door. It was a walk that he had obviously practiced and, to his satisfaction, perfected, and it was meant to intimidate and awe any who were privileged to see it.

Officer Murray Evans had been on the job with the Nacogdoches Police Department exactly two months. It was his first week to be on solo night patrol, and this night had been a rousing success. He had already issued three citations for alcohol possession by a minor and had called for one car to be towed and its inebriated driver to be taken to the city jail. It seemed to Officer Evans that the kids these days had no respect for the law, especially on homecoming weekend; but Officer Murray Evans was going to make them wish they did!

"You wanta step outta that car," the officer said. It was not a question. The door opened and a young black man stepped out. He was nicely dressed: black slacks and white shirt, a bright yellow tie, and a gray sports coat with a small flower on the lapel. E.J. Campbell, the black high school in town, was holding its homecoming dance that evening. It appeared to Pastor Dexter as if the young man had just come from that dance.

"You been to homecoming tonight?" the officer asked as the young man handed over his driver's license.

"Yes suh," the young man replied. His voice was trembling with anxiety.

"This your car?"

"It's my father's car, suh."

"And he just let you take it out tonight," the officer said with mock disbelief. He seemed to be enjoying the exchange.

"Yes suh; I'm supposed to be home before midnight."

"I'll bet your daddy wouldn't be real happy to know that you was drinking and driving tonight, now would he?"

The young man's eyes grew wide with disbelief. "Oh no suh, I'd nevah do that."

"Now you mean to tell me that you went to a homecoming dance and no one there was passin' around a flask or a bottle or a can of somethin'? Do you really want me to believe that?"

"Some of the fellas was takin' a sip or two, but I never did!"

"So you're the one fella who didn't take a sip tonight." The officer snickered to himself and scanned the young man's driver's license with his flashlight. "I am sure privileged to be speaking to the one fella who didn't take a drink tonight," he mumbled to himself as he read.

"You Elijah Wilson?"

"Yes, suh."

"Says here you live over on Shawnee; whacha doin' all the way over here on Park Street?"

"I was takin' my date home; she stays on the next street down."

Officer Evans seemed surprised by the revelation. It seems he had forgotten the "always check the car for other occupants" directive from his training days at the academy. He directed his light into the car and he and Pastor Dexter saw for the first time a neatly dressed young lady sitting in the passenger's seat, her head facing forward and her hands folded in her lap.

"And you mean to tell me..." the officer began, but he stopped when he saw Elijah's eyes focused on something behind him. Officer Evans turned and saw for the first time what Elijah had recently discovered, that someone was standing a few feet away, watching as events unfolded.

"Sir, you're gonna need to move inside while I take care of this matter here." Certain that his uniform and authoritative voice had done the trick, the officer turned his attention back to Elijah.

"I'm gonna ask you to open your trunk 'cause I have a sneaking suspicion that you have a bottle or two in there; and when I find that bottle and it becomes clear that you was lyin' to me, I'm gonna…" But Officer Evans' voice trailed off again when he saw that Elijah was still looking over his shoulder.

The man was still there! Officer Murray Evans was dumbfounded. His unmistakably clear order had been disregarded.

"Sir, I said you're gonna have to get in your house. I have this matter well in hand." But this time, instead of turning back to Elijah, Officer Evans continued to face Pastor Dexter, waiting for him to move.

Pastor Dexter had all the respect in the world for the Nacogdoches Police Department. He had ridden along on patrol on several occasions and had even served as a chaplain-on-call for emergencies. But he did not feel right about leaving Elijah Wilson without a witness. As he looked into Elijah's eyes, he thought he sensed an unspoken plea, asking him to stay right where he was. And so he didn't move.

"Now sir, I don't want to have to deal with you, too. I can't tell you how hard the judge comes down on someone that interferes with police business. He takes it right personal."

Pastor Dexter finally spoke. "I'm simply standing in my yard, officer, not bothering anyone, not interfering with anything. I believe I have the right to do that. So feel free to continue your discussion with Mr. Wilson and his date and I'll just stay right here and won't say a word."

At that point, Officer Evans realized that this individual had heard all that had been going on, that he knew names and details, that he knew much more than the good officer felt comfortable with him knowing.

Turning back to Elijah, he handed him back his driver's license and said with as much authority as he could muster, "You just make sure you keep your drivin' and your drinkin' on opposite nights, 'cause I'll be on patrol to make sure you do. Do we understand each other?"

"Yes, suh," Elijah answered.

"Well, go on." Officer Evans waved Elijah back into his car and it slowly pulled away.

Turning to Pastor Dexter he said in his most intimidating voice, "The chief is going to hear about this, mister, and you're gonna wish you had moved inside when I asked you. Name?"

"Donald Dexter, 519 Park Street."

The officer wrote in his notepad, walked back to his patrol car and drove away.

"He basically said he was going to talk to the chief and that I would be sorry I didn't go inside." Donald Dexter stood in front of the mirror and worked on his Windsor knot for the third and hopefully the last time.

"Are you sure you did the right thing, staying out there when a policeman told you not to?" Mrs. Dexter's concern showed on her pretty face.

"Sweetheart, it's my right as an American to stand in my own front yard. In Nazi Germany, citizens couldn't stand in their own front yards, but that's why we fought the war!" Pastor Dexter's voice was strong and confident, but inside he was wishing he felt as confident as he sounded.

"I think you've been watching too many episodes of *Perry Mason*," his wife mumbled as she left the bedroom to check on lunch preparations.

Pastor Dexter, who heard every word, mumbled back so that only he could hear, "First of all, it's impossible to watch too many episodes of *Perry Mason*; best dad-gum show on television. And secondly, if you had seen that young man's face, you would have stayed, too. I know you would have."

As he gathered his notes and his Bible and headed for the office, Pastor Dexter recalled an incident from the third grade. He had taken an apple from Bobbie Sue Clifton's lunch bucket and replaced it with a turnip. The substitute teacher had learned of the deed and told the trembling third grader that she was informing Mr. O'Malley, the principal. "You'll be hearing from him soon."

Donald Dexter was a World War II veteran, the winner of a Purple Heart and the USAF Flying Medal, a college graduate, a seminary valedictorian, a pastor, a husband, and a father of three. But on this particular morning, he felt much more like that fearful third grader, quaking at his desk, waiting for the principal to call.

As Pastor Dexter rose to speak that November morning, another pastor across town was beginning his sermon, as well.

"My text for the morning is from the Book of Amos, Chapter 5, verses 23 and 24." In a strong and somber pulpit voice, he read. "Take away from Me the noise of your songs, for I will not hear the melody of your stringed instruments. But let justice roll down like water, and righteousness like a mighty stream."

"I have a question to ask this morning, my precious brothers and sisters. It is a question that God himself asks of his people time and time again. And why did He ask it time and time again?"

The congregation began to feel a wave of emotion rising, and they joined in the surge. *Tell us, pastor, tell us.*

"Was it because Israel had forgotten what the Lord had said?"

No brother, that's not the reason.

"Did somebody simply forget to write down those holy words?"

They wrote 'em, pastor, they wrote 'em.

"Or did God repeat Himself over and over because Israel refused to change?"

That's the truth of it; that's the truth.

"After the first time they heard it..."

They didn't change.

"And the second time they heard it..."

No difference at all.

"And the third time they heard it?"

The wave of emotion crashed over the congregation as everyone agreed that Israel had failed to heed God's Word.

"I want a pure people." The pastor spoke as if God was speaking.

Amen.

"I don't want your tithes unless your heart comes along with them; I don't want your songs without a spirit that's broken before Me; I don't want buildings of brick and wood, I want buildings of flesh and blood." The congregation was following, phrase by phrase and word by word.

"You think God wants a pile of money?"

No, no.

"You think He dreams at night about Sunday School attendance numbers?"

No, pastor, no.

"You think God mopes around Heaven wishing His people would build him a few more grand churches?"

The congregation was indignant that anyone would think so.

"Listen to what God wants." He held his well-worn Bible before him and prepared to read the text again. The congregation grew silent before the reading of the Word of God.

"But let justice roll down like water, and righteousness like a mighty stream." He spoke the words with a quiet, measured voice as if offering evening vespers.

"That's what God wants – for me and you, for this church, for this community, for this nation." Somber *Amens* followed with quiet pleas of *Yes, Lord* and *Please, God.*

"Black folks in this country are ready for something new on the menu; they're ready for a plate piled high with Justice." The congregation hummed their agreement. "And if you don't mind, we'll take a side order of Righteousness with that, please!" Some laughed, but all affirmed the desire. "And would anyone appreciate some fresh baked Mercy with a little hot, melted Kindness on top?" The crowd roared their enthusiastic approval. Pastor Jeremiah Wilson brought the tone down to a whisper. "And I'd like to wash it all down with a tall, cold glass of iced Peace."

And then the good pastor did what he had never done in twelve years of preaching. He stepped away from the pulpit, away from the place of authority, and moved down off the platform until he was standing in the center aisle, not five feet from the nearest parishioner.

"I want to speak to you for a moment as your neighbor and friend, as a husband, and as a father." As he said those last words, his eyes fell on his son, Elijah Wilson, who was sitting next to his mother on the front row.

"My son, Elijah, was stopped last night on his way home from the homecoming dance. The officer said he had been drinking and driving." There was some mumbling in the congregation. "But he was not! My son is not perfect, but last night, he was fairly close to it." Some chuckles followed.

"The officer was giving him a hard time, and I think you know why." More mumbling.

"Brothers and sisters, it's been like that all my life, and it's never gonna change until more than Black hearts are broken by the injustice, until more than Black heads are bowed in prayer asking God to show us His righteousness." Amens throughout.

"I'm happy to tell you, brothers and sisters," tears were forming in the corners of Pastor Wilson's eyes, "that last night, a man stood in the gap for my son. He stood watch to make sure no evil transpired; he refused to leave when told to…" he let the impact of those words sink in, "…because of his concern for my son, Elijah." Tears were rolling down his cheeks as he continued.

"That brave individual was not one of Elijah's classmates; it was not even one of you, though I know you would have been there if it meant helping out my son." *Amen.*

"It was a White man, brothers and sisters." It was pin-drop silent in the church. "It was a pastor of a white church by the name of Donald Dexter, a man of God who pastors the First Christian Church, the church situated across from the White high school's gym." Everyone recognized the church.

"It's been like this all my life…but maybe, just maybe things are changing. When a White man stands up to another White man for the sake of a young Black man…well then maybe, just maybe things are changing."

That afternoon, Pastor Dexter sat in front of his television set and watched the Green Bay Packers methodically take apart the Dallas Cowboys for their eighth consecutive loss of the season. He saw the distraught coach, Tom Landry, on the sidelines, but he couldn't seem to muster an ounce of sympathy for him. He was back in the third-grader-waiting-for-the-principal-to-call mood and just couldn't seem to shake it.

It was well past 1:00 a.m. before he finally fell asleep that night.

Mondays were usually casual days for Pastor Donald Dexter. He filed his sermons, recorded Sunday School and Worship attendance and offering numbers in his pastoral record book, planned his weekly schedule, caught up on the stack of mail from the previous week, and did some reading from the latest issue of *Christianity Today.*

But as casual and relaxed as Pastor Dexter tried to make the day, his stomach wouldn't cooperate with the idea, twisted into a perpetual knot as he waited for his office phone to ring. Ever since the confrontation with Officer Evans on Saturday night, he had imagined and lived through a variety of scenarios, each more embarrassing and devastating than the one before. In his most recent imagining, a police car actually pulled up in front of the church office; and while the young pastor was taken away in handcuffs, countless prominent Nacogdoches citizens and the entire congregation of First Christian Church were on hand to witness his humiliation. That one woke him from his sleep, but unlike most nightmares, it refused to dissolve away with the new day.

Pastor Dexter was down the hall from his office, checking the toilet paper supply for the men's and women's restrooms when his office phone rang. He was back down the hall, in his office, and seated behind his desk by the third ring, a roll of toilet paper still in his hand.

He took a deep breath and tried to sound as matter-of-fact as possible. "First Christian Church, Donald Dexter speaking."

The woman's voice at the other end was all business. "This is Regina Henty, Chief Stanton's secretary. Is this Pastor Donald Dexter of the First Christian Church?"

Pastor Dexter was momentarily tempted to remind Miss Henty to actually listen when someone answered the phone, but he quickly thought better of it. "Yes, ma'am," he replied. The "ma'am" was partly from his Southern upbringing and partly because Miss Henty sounded like someone his mother's age.

"Chief Stanton would like a moment of your time." There was a click followed by an electronic buzzing. Another click, and then a smooth, slow, bass voice on the other end of the line.

"Pastor Dexter, this is Roger Stanton of the Nacogdoches Police Department. Thank you for taking my call this morning."

"Of course," Pastor Dexter replied. His heart was racing and he could feel droplets of sweat running down his sides.

"I have in my office this morning one of our newest officers, Officer Murray Evans."

"Dear God," Pastor Dexter thought, "he actually reported me!"

"He's given me a full report of what transpired last Saturday night on Park Street. I've asked him a few additional questions, and I believe I have a fairly complete picture of all that took place."

Pastor Dexter was waiting for the hammer to fall when the chief continued. "At this time, Officer Evans would like to speak to you himself."

There was a thumping as the receiver was passed from one to the other, a few hushed words between the men, and then a much subdued Officer Evans on the other end of the line.

"Pastor Dexter, this is Murray Evans of the Nacogdoches Police Department. We met the other night in front of your house on Park Street?"

"Yes, I recall." He tried to sound as if the meeting had almost slipped his mind.

"I just wanted to tell you personally, sir, how sorry I am for my behavior on that night." Pastor Dexter couldn't believe what he was hearing. "We have been trained to treat every citizen with respect and dignity, and I'm afraid I did a poor job in that regard on Saturday night."

There was some more muffled conversation between the two police officers and then Officer Evans continued.

"The chief and I have discussed the matter and we agree that you would be well within your rights to file a complaint against me regarding the matter. I'll hand the phone back to the chief now."

Pastor Dexter tried to imagine the "discussion" the two men had and the ultimatums that were issued before the "agreement" was reached.

"Pastor Dexter, this is Chief Stanton again. I'm fairly sure we have us an excellent officer in the making with young Evans here. But like all rookies, he's gonna make a few mistakes before he gets both feet solid into police work. I'll bet you've even made a few rookie mistakes as a pastor, am I right?"

"More than a few, I'm afraid." There was a lighthearted tone to Pastor Dexter's voice.

"So we've had us a conversation this morning and we've reached some conclusions together. But if you would like to make a formal complaint against Officer Evans, you are certainly free to do that."

"Oh, no sir. I'm sure you've dealt with the matter quite thoroughly."

"Well thank you, Pastor Dexter, for your understanding. I'm sure this is the last conversation of this type the three of us will ever need to have."

Pastor Dexter was on the verge of agreeing with the good chief when a click and a buzzing at the other end of the line told him the conversation was over.

He could have called, but instead he ran to the parsonage to tell Vennie what had just happened.

TOM AND THE GIRL HATERS CLUB

Tom Pruitt's older brother Ken drove Bus #83. Ken had played football for the NHS Dragons the year before and Kyle and Tom had cheered from the stands each time his name was announced, and it was announced often. But his glory years on the gridiron had ended, and Ken was making his way through his freshman year at SFA, in part, by driving Bus #83.

The first months on Bus #83 were months of privilege. After all, who was going to mess with Kyle when he was best friends with the bus driver's brother? Tom, who rode the bus a good 30 minutes before it picked up Kyle, had the back two seats saved for himself and anyone he chose to honor on any particular day. There was no bullying involved, no threats or angry words, just a universally understood axiom of ownership for the bus driver's brother. And no matter who might or might not be chosen for backseat privileges on a given day, Kyle was always certain that Tom had saved the seat next to himself for his good friend.

And so every morning, for the fifteen-minute ride between Kyle's bus stop and Raguet Elementary's front door, Tom and Kyle exchanged stories, jokes, and snippets of the homework that was due a few hours later. The bus ride was, for those first weeks, a safe and privileged experience.

Then one day the bus doors opened and Kyle saw that Ken was smiling at him with an unusually mischievous smile, and that made Kyle uneasy. As he climbed the steps into the bus he began to see that everyone onboard was smiling that same unnerving smile. What did they all know that he didn't?

It was Ken who spoke the punch line. "Walk a mile, Kyle," he said, and everyone exploded in laughter. Ken had thought of the line and had announced to the bus riders that it would be given a test run that very morning. Based on Kyle's surprised look and the hearty laughter of his fellow bus riders, the joke was declared to be a winner.

"He's just messin' with ya," Tom told him when he finally reached the back seat. "He thought of it the other evening at the dinner table, and Dad laughed so hard that he just had to try it out for real."

The next day and the day after and the day after that Ken greeted Kyle with a big smile and a hearty, "Walk a mile, Kyle!" And as he walked the aisle to the backseat, Kyle had to admit that it felt like a mile, easy! And each time he passed a row of seats, at least one of the occupants would add his own, "Walk a mile, Kyle," to the roast.

And so day after day Kyle was the butt of the morning and afternoon joke on Bus #83, and it probably would have stayed that way until Christmas break if Mrs. Dexter had not found out about it.

One afternoon Kyle dragged into the kitchen looking a bit beaten down. Mrs. Dexter kept one eye on the pork chops sizzling in the cast iron skillet and the other eye on Kyle.

As he did almost every day after school, Kyle cupped his hand under the kitchen faucet and drank his fill of the cool, clean water. He wiped his hand on his jeans and started for his bedroom when his mother asked, "Everything all right, Kyle?" Her eyes were on the pork chops, but he knew she was listening.

"Yeah, it's nothing really," he began, "It's just that some of the kids on the bus have something they say every time I get on or off the bus."

Kyle looked at his mother and noted that she was no longer worrying about the pork chops. She lifted the heavy skillet off the gas flames and set it aside. The sizzling and popping noises began to subside as Mrs. Dexter sat on the tall, red kitchen stool, looked Kyle in the eyes and said, "And what is it they say?"

"Walk a mile, Kyle." There, he had said it for the first time himself and he realized when he said it out loud that not only did it not sound mean or hurtful, but it actually sounded innocent and silly. So what was he so upset about?

But Mrs. Dexter knew exactly what he was upset about. She had been thin and small growing up and had heard enough silly names like "Chicken Legs" and enough funny names like "Sticks" to know that there was nothing silly or funny about them.

Kyle had seen his mother's lips pressed into a straight line before, and he knew she meant business. When there was an injustice to be righted or a great evil to be confronted, Mrs. Dexter was an unyielding warrior-queen, especially when it pertained to family matters.

Moments later, as she stirred the gravy in the pan before her, she continued to question Kyle.

"So Ken Pruitt says it first, does he?"

"Yes, Ma'am."

"And it happens every day?"

"Twice a day."

On many occasions, the gravy at the Dexter dinner table had lumps, though it could hardly be called lumpy. But on this specific evening, the gravy was stirred with such vigor and the lumps were attacked with such righteous anger that the finished product was worthy of a table at Delmonico's. Kyle's dad even commented on how exceptional the gravy was that evening.

As she put away the evening dishes, Mrs. Dexter's mind roamed the Universe for a solution to Kyle's dilemma. He could ride to school with Donna and her friends, but he would never hear the end of it if he took the coward's way out. Or she could walk her son to the bus stop and confront the situation head-on, but if she did, Kyle would have to find a new life under an assumed name in a new city.

The Scripture reading for the previous week's Sunday School lesson had been Romans 12:19, "'VENGEANCE IS MINE, I WILL REPAY,' says the Lord." Not only could Mrs. Dexter not get the verse out of her head, but she had even been chosen to read the text in front of the whole class. It, therefore, seemed doubly unsuitable to suggest that Kyle take some kind of physical action the next time the verbal bullying began.

Wishing that the Lord was more visibly on Bus #83 and that his vengeance didn't have to wait until Judgment Day, Mrs. Dexter continued to search for a solution.

And as she emptied the sink, a thought began to gently glow in her mind. As she dried her hands on a dishtowel the idea became more distinct, and by the time she was spreading the dishtowel over the kitchen faucet, the solution to Kyle's problem was obvious and complete, bathed in the light of creative inspiration and motherly love.

That night, before bed, Mrs. Dexter took Kyle aside and whispered her inspiration in his ear. If she had any doubts about her plan, they evaporated in the light of Kyle's smile and the surge of relief that softened his face and relaxed his shoulders.

The sun seemed especially warm that next morning and the birds seemed unusually active and in great voice. At least that's how it seemed to Kyle and his mother as they ate their Malt-O-Meal and got ready for the day.

"Have a good day," Mrs. Dexter said as Kyle opened the front door. Kyle paused, looked at his mother with a beaming smile and replied, "Oh, I will!"

Bus #83 rolled up right on time, but there was no dread in Kyle's heart as the doors swung open. Instead of praying, as he had in the days past, that Ken would finally forget his morning salutation, Kyle prayed that he wouldn't. He was not disappointed.

"Walk a mile, Kyle", Ken said with a good-natured grin. Kyle was almost breathless with anticipation. When he spoke, the words were a bit too loud and his voice was unusually high-pitched, but he got the words out nonetheless: "You do it, Pruitt!"

There was a moment of dead silence in which Kyle wondered if Mrs. Dexter's plan was going to work. But the silence was quickly broken with peals of laughter. Ken, who it turns out, could take it as well as he could dish it out, could not control his hilarity.

When his fit of laughter finally stopped, Ken repeated the words out loud, "You do it, Pruitt," just so he could revisit the sound of them, and the laughter began again.

From that day forward, Ken and Kyle had a friendly verbal joust as Kyle got on and off the bus each day."

"Walk a mile, Kyle."

"You do it, Pruitt."

And the two would laugh, and the universe was in harmony once again.

The topics of conversation at the back of Bus #83 shifted as dramatically as the East Texas weather. But one topic that almost always made the cut was the Three Stooges episodes from the afternoon before. One of the Shreveport channels showed back-to-back Three Stooges episodes on weekday afternoons, and Tom and Kyle never missed. One episode, however, would seize their imaginations and not let go until it had given their lives a vigorous and unneighborly shaking.

"I can't believe they had a Woman Haters Club with an initiation, a pledge, a flag and everything," Tom said as he and Kyle reflected on all things Stooge.

"You know what we need, don't you; we need a Girl Haters Club for the guys in Mrs. Hartsfield's room!"

Who actually said those words became a matter of discussion and disagreement as the days progressed. Tom was almost sure it was Kyle's idea, and Kyle was nearly certain that the idea had originated with Tom.

But regardless of its source, the inspirational seed began to grow in each boy's imagination. "You come up with the initiation and the pledge," Tom said breathlessly, "and I'll write the charter and bring the flag."

On the playground that afternoon the two misogynists shared their creative vision. "We'll bring the charter tomorrow; you can only join The Girl Haters Club after you pass the initiation, recite the pledge and sign your name to the charter. Then you're in."

There was universal enthusiasm among the boys of 4A. Kyle and Tom had been recognized as the captain and first mate of the concept, and both went home determined to reward the faith of their classmates.

If either Kyle or Tom had worked half as hard on Math or Geography or Science or Social Studies as they worked on their part of the Girl Haters Club, they most likely would have skipped 5th grade altogether and jumped directly into 6th.

Both were impressed as they compared notes the next day on the back of the bus.

"Initiation into the Girl Haters Club," Kyle read. "To be eligible for membership in the Girl Haters Club, you must walk within five feet of Betty or

Larka or Debbie all by yourself without saying a word. If they speak to you, you must remain silent."

"Perfect," Tom said, "that'll show who's brave and who's not."

"Pledge of a Girl Hater," Kyle continued. "I, then you have to say your name, promise that I will not talk to a girl in 4A, sit next to a girl in 4A or be the boyfriend of a girl in 4A. And you have to raise your right hand when you say it."

"Perfect again," Tom said. "And here's the charter."

Tom pulled out a long piece of paper with a dowel glued to each end. The paper had been rolled into what looked like a proclamation from an episode of *The Adventures of Robin Hood*. He carefully unrolled the scroll, held it ceremoniously at arm's length and began to read.

"Let it be known," Tom began in his most melodramatic voice, "that all the undersigned are members in good standing with the Nacogdoches Chapter of the Girl Haters Club, International, Troop 4A."

There were enough lines on the bottom of the scroll to accommodate signatures from each of the guys in Mrs. Hartsfield's room.

And the signatures started rolling in that afternoon. Lunchtime provided the perfect opportunity for the initiation. Potential members tingled with excitement as they were required to walk with their trays past Betty or Larka or Debbie while the girls ate their lunches. And the excitement began to grow as each initiate raised his right hand and solemnly stated the Pledge of a Girl Hater. But the excitement overflowed at recess when each signed the Charter and stood together under Tom's flag. The flag was not really a flag; it was, in essence, the remnant of a roll of butcher paper that could be telescoped to a height of about eight feet, but it was enough of a flag to show members where to run for safety and solidarity should a girl come close or try to speak to them.

Tom suggested that a real club has properly elected officers and takes up regular dues, but discussion on those matters was interrupted by the bell that ended recess. As Tom and Kyle analyzed the day on their afternoon bus ride home, they both agreed that the Nacogdoches Chapter of The Girl Haters Club, International was off to one heck of a start!

The next day was a Friday, by far the best day of the week! There would be an extended show-and-tell session to begin the day, there would be fish sticks for lunch thanks to the Catholics in the school, and there would be free play for recess, a perfect time for The Girl Haters Club to meet and conduct some much-needed business.

Show-and-tell started out with a joke. Dan and Tom and Kyle had done the joke in 3rd grade, but it was due for a command performance.

Dan started and delivered his lines with the required boastfulness. "My dad owns the movie theater, and I can get in for nothing!"

Tom followed. "Oh yeah, my dad's a doctor and I can be sick for nothing."

Kyle had the punch line. "So what; my dad's a preacher and I can be good for nothing!"

The room roared its approval as it had the year before. One reason the joke worked so well was that Dan's father actually did manage one of the local theaters, Tom's father was a doctor, and Kyle's dad was a preacher.

"Who would like to go next?" Mrs. Hartsfield did her best to keep the action moving; unlike her students, she was still considering the possibility of some actual learning taking place before the final bell sounded.

At this bright moment, when smiles were still on 4A's faces and an entire day of good things stretched before them, a cloud passed over the sun. Show and Tell suddenly and tragically became Show and Tattletale.

One girl rose and walked to the front of the room. "Some of the boys have a club called The Girl Haters Club and they think it's funny to be mean to the girls."

The first girl sat down and a second rose to take her place. "And if we talk to them, they will get kicked out of the club if they say something back to us."

As the second girl headed for her seat, the remaining contributors didn't even bother to leave their seats as they spoke out one after the other.

"They have a pledge where they promise to hate girls."

"And they have a piece of paper that everyone signed."

"And they won't sit by us at lunch."

"And Kyle's the president."

"And Tom has a flag."

There it was; the ugly truth had been told; their dirty laundry had been hung out to dry and everyone could see their unmentionables. Kyle could feel his ears burning and his face on fire with embarrassment. He glanced at Tom and saw that he was fidgeting nervously, pulling on a string that hung from his blue jeans. Their names had been mentioned, but at least they were still arm-in-arm with their fellow club members.

"I didn't sign the charter; I thought it was a bad idea." One of the once-enthusiastic Girl Haters was trying to weasel out of his uncomfortable predicament.

"I just thought it was a fun club; I didn't know anything about hating girls." Another Girl Hater, seeing his classmate reach apparent safety from the sinking ship, jumped for a passing piece of flotsam.

"Me either," said one.

"Me either," said another who thought it sounded convincing enough.

"Kyle and Tom came up with the idea."

There it was – the final nail in the coffin. The silence that followed the statement has been referred to in similar settings as 'the silence of ascent'. Not only had the girls tattled, but the boys had gone along for the ride. The vessel was slowly but surely sinking and the rats were disembarking at an alarming clip.

Mrs. Hartsfield stood and said a few words about how all her students needed to be careful of the feelings of others and that she was certain that 4A had seen the last of The Girl Haters Club.

And so a Friday full of potential was once again ruined. There was an uneasy feeling between Tom and Kyle and all the other boys of 4A. Tom and Kyle ate lunch together, isolated from the rest of the class; no one seemed to want to be too close to the radioactive duo.

Kyle avoided eye contact with Mrs. Hartsfield. He knew he had disappointed her, had let her down. He also knew that she would be sitting in the choir on Sunday morning on the same row as his mother. Maybe the consequences were over for Tom, but Kyle imagined that they were just beginning for him.

That afternoon before recess, Kyle glanced around the room and noticed that Debbie was looking at him intently. Debbie, who in the 1st grade had been so happy that he had come. Debbie, who in the 2nd grade made the whole class laugh when she asked the teacher out loud if she could sit next to Kyle. Debbie, who in the 3rd grade sent Kyle a Valentine's Day card that said, "I love you, Debbie" inside a hand-drawn heart.

How often had Kyle pushed her away in one form or another? How often had he spurned her simple acts of kindness or rejected her more open demonstrations of affection?

As he looked at Debbie, he noticed that her eyes were wide with intensity and wet with emotion. Her head was tilted to one side and her lower lip was thrust out as evidence of her great disappointment in Kyle. Kyle had hurt her feelings before, and he had more than once refused her less than subtle invitations to friendship. But this time, he had broken her heart.

Kyle Dexter was President of the Nacogdoches Chapter of The Girl Haters Club, International, and Debbie, he realized with a sinking heart, was one of the girls he claimed to hate. Looking into the face of a sweet girl who had only wanted to give Kyle her affection, he felt, once again, the great weight of shame in his life.

Saturday was one of the longest days Kyle had ever known. He kept waiting for someone to ring the doorbell and deliver a telegram, like they did in the old movies, which would inform his parents of his great shame. Every time the phone rang, and it rang a half-dozen times, Kyle would think of some excuse for sauntering past the phone extension at the foot of the stairs in order to determine if Mrs. Hartsfield was on the other end of the line. His best Peter Gunn impersonation led him to conclude that no such phone call was made.

Then came Sunday morning. Mrs. Hartsfield and Mrs. Dexter were in the same Sunday School class and then together again in the choir room where they put on their robes. There would be plenty of opportunity for the whole sordid Girl Haters story to be related.

The service began; the choir and Pastor Dexter made their entrance.

Hymns were sung, prayers said, offerings taken. Finally Pastor Dexter settled into his message. Kyle kept his eyes on his father, not wanting to let them drift to Mrs. Hartsfield or his mother.

He could imagine two pairs of eyes glaring daggers at him, two frowning and disappointed faces, two ladies who wanted to stand in unison and say to this hater of girls, "We used to be girls too you know!"

Finally his desire to know weighed heavier than his fear of finding out. Kyle's gaze shifted ever so slowly to his left until it rested on his mother. Her gaze was on her husband, and it was the same look of pride and admiration that Kyle saw each week. Not only was she not thinking that Kyle was a future felon, she wasn't thinking of Kyle at all!

Taking a deep breath Kyle moved his eyes still further left until they rested on Mrs. Hartsfield only to discover that her eyes were already resting on him, and she was smiling. Not the sinister smile of the person who knows your darkest secrets and has ultimate mischief in mind, but rather the kind, beneficent smile of one who knows all there is to know about you and yet still loves you. Kyle smiled back and Mrs. Hartsfield's smile grew, and Kyle immediately knew: "She's not going to tell; she's not going to tell!"

The thing settled between them, Kyle and his teacher turned their attention to Pastor Dexter and listened to his message.

THE HOOTING WOMAN

There are certain days in Nacogdoches that are nothing short of magical, when every facet of the day reflects excitement and fuels enthusiasm and whispers the promise of wondrous things to come. A particular Saturday in November was one of those days.

All day Friday a strong wind had blown from the north. There were cold showers and dark skies. But the cold, gloomy Friday night gave way to a blue-skied Saturday morning, cool and apple-crisp.

Kyle felt the chilly breeze on his resting form and he smiled. He turned on his belly, put his chin on his folded arms, and watched out his open window as the sunlight danced through the brown and dying leaves. Dozens, scores, hundreds of oak leaves had given up their fight to hang on and were floating on the breeze and coming to rest in the Dexter front yard. The scene foretold hours of hard work to come – raking and hauling and burning, but that would be on another day, not this one.

And as he watched, Kyle intuitively became aware of what generations of fourth grade boys had known before him, that falling leaves are not meant to be watched; they are meant to be caught! In a burst of delicious urgency, Kyle slipped into his jeans, his SFA sweatshirt, and tennis shoes and was out the back door and into the new day. He couldn't have stayed inside if he had wanted to. He ran with the breeze and against it, into the sunlight and back into the shade, chasing and catching leaves as they fell.

A day would come all too soon when catching leaves would be considered childish, when Kyle would be too self-conscious to run through the falling leaves, too worried that one of his friends would see him and laugh at him. But that day had not yet arrived. The perfect day had converged with the perfect age, and Kyle revelled in their fortuitous intersection.

Mrs. Dexter looked out the kitchen window as she mixed the Saturday pancake batter. She had seen in her youth how calves and foals kicked up their heels on days such as this one, apparently overwhelmed with the joy of being alive. As she watched Kyle frolic in the morning light, she smiled, remembering other days – leaf-catching, cold-on-your-ears, run-'til-you-drop days. She stirred the batter and watched her son and remembered, and he frolicked for the two of them.

It didn't take Kyle long to learn that catching leaves on the wind was nothing like playing left field in little league. Unlike the baseball's predictable flight, leaves in the breeze jerked and halted, dashed and dropped so that catching one was a most satisfying accomplishment.

Catching leaves soon became, in Kyle's mind, a life-or-death drama. Instead of leaves he was catching, it was beautiful girls he was saving from eminent death. He named them as they fell: Debbie, Betty, Joy, Teri, Larka, Katherine. Kyle could see the troubled faces of his comely classmates as they fell; he could hear their cries for help. He threw himself wildly to the ground to catch and protect those damsels in distress.

And with every courageous and sacrificial rescue, Kyle imagined the grateful smiles and the tearful words of thanks. And just the thought of those tender smiles and tender words caused his stomach to ache in that new and deliciously sweet way, and for such a sensation, a scuffed knee and a few grass stains were a small price to pay.

When his ears and fingers were numbed from the cold, Kyle ran for home and warmth and Saturday morning pancakes.

"Where's Ricky?" he asked his mom as he hurried through the kitchen. Ricky loved his Saturday morning rest, and it was most unusual for him to be up earlier than Kyle.

"He's with George, trying out his new rifle." A lot of eighth grade guys talked about girls and sports, but Ricky and his one-street-over friend, George, talked about guns.

After setting aside his lawn mowing money for several months, Ricky had ordered a British Enfield .303 rifle from the back pages of a "Guns & Ammo" magazine. The whole family had seen the rifle in action that past Saturday evening as they watched "Desert Rats" on *Saturday Night at the Movies*.

"That's the rifle I ordered!" Ricky pointed out enthusiastically as the British infantry charged across the desert sands. And now he was in George's back pasture making dozens of bottles and cans rue the day they had ever enlisted in the Fuehrer's cause.

"Wheat or plain?" Mrs. Dexter asked.

"Plain," Kyle answered, "but make it in a funny shape."

Kyle ran to the living room and stood before the hissing gas space heater, turning his back to the heat until his pants were painfully hot to the touch and then turning around slowly like a roast on a spit so that he would be evenly done when the turning was complete.

Kyle watched as the gas flames licked the stalactite covered bricks on the back of the stove. They glowed in shades of red and white and blue and orange and yellow. As the flames danced up and down, the colors shifted and blended so that Kyle was hypnotized by the fiery kaleidoscope and its mesmerizing hiss. His vision blurred into a sea of colors, and he was lost in a world of delight, an enchanted world of cool breezes, warm fires and pancakes on the way.

"Your pancake's ready," Mrs. Dexter called out from the kitchen. She proudly displayed her culinary creation – a circle with two smaller circles on the upper left and right.

"Mickey!" Kyle exclaimed. "Thanks, Mom."

Eating his mother's pancakes was always a treat, but eating a pancake in the shape of Mickey Mouse made it especially delicious.

As Kyle finished the last bites of his syrup-soaked Mickey, Ricky and George burst through the front door, laughing uncontrollably.

"Come upstairs," they cried as they bounded up the stairs two at a time. By the time Kyle reached the bedroom, the boys were laying side-by-side on Ricky's bed, looking out the window and waiting for something.

"Lie down," Ricky said, "just watch out the window – and keep quiet!" Kyle watched and waited but saw nothing out of the ordinary.

Suddenly Kyle remembered a similar experience from the summer before, a "snipe hunt" Ricky's Boy Scout troop had organized for Kyle's Cub Scout pack. He recalled the hours he and the other Cubs had waited, burlap bags open, anxious for the snipe that would soon hear their unique whistles and stumble into the traps. But, of course, nothing came except the uncontrollable laughter of the older boys.

Kyle was wondering if he was being similarly duped when Ricky whispered, "Here she comes."

Down Park Street towards Logansport and just coming into view was an ancient, diminutive woman. Kyle was short for his age, but he would have towered over the tiny figure if they had stood toe-to-toe. This would not have been the case if the old woman had stood up straight, but standing straight was apparently something she had been unable to do for years.

The tiny woman was almost bent at a right angle, giving the appearance that she was inspecting with great care her every next step or that she was possibly looking for loose change that she had dropped in days past.

The floral print of her dress was from Kyle's grandmother's generation; the once bright flowers had been in early bloom decades before but now appeared tired and faded from too many scrubbings in the kitchen sink and too many hours drying in the bright East Texas sunlight.

The dress had obviously been purchased for someone else; it hung on the stooped woman like Mrs. Dexter's dresses hung on Donna when she played "dress-up". Only there seemed to be none of Donna's joy in the old woman's face.

As Kyle looked at the ill-fitting dress again, a thought came to him. What if the dress had been purchased for the old lady during a time in which it fit her? What if she had been tall and straight and beautiful once and the dress had fit her to a tee? What if men in decades past had turned their heads when she passed in the floral print, enjoying a second look and praying that she would turn her head for an intoxicating second look at them? But as the old woman continued her painfully difficult progress down Park Street, the thought of a once beautiful lady seemed like so much fantasy.

In her right hand and hanging loosely at her side was an empty canvas bag. Her left hand was on her abdomen, in Napoleonic fashion. There was a "clip, clop, clip, clop" as her shoes struck the sidewalk with a brisk intensity. "Clip, clop" was the sound that wooden shoes made in stories from Geography class about little Dutch boys and girls, but it was also, as Kyle observed, the sound that shoes make when they are several sizes too large and are straining to come off with every step.

On top of the old woman's head was an immense volume of gray hair, carelessly swirled and twirled and pinned with a hundred bobby pins. The pile of gray seemed to double her height and intensify her disheveled appearance. In spite of someone's tireless efforts, dozens of sprigs of hair were moving with the cool breeze, asserting their independence and refusing to conform to the old lady's design.

Directly in front of the Dexter house, the rapid-fire slapping of her shoes abruptly stopped. This was what Ricky and George had been waiting for. "Hoot, hoot", the old woman cried in a loud, piercing voice. She started down the sidewalk for a few more steps, stopped and hooted again, then continued on her way.

Ricky and George were shaking with laughter, their faces buried in the pillow so as not to be heard by the hooting woman.

"Did she just hoot?" Kyle asked.

"She does it all the time", Ricky said in between seizures of convulsive laughter. "We think she must be crazy; she thinks she's an owl or something."

Ricky and George ran down the stairs to find other distractions and Kyle was left alone with his thoughts. He was immediately uncomfortable with the thought of a crazy woman walking by his house on a regular basis. What if she walked by at night? What if she did more than hoot? What if she not only thought she was an owl but also thought that Kyle looked a lot like a mouse?

Kyle wanted to see the old woman again from the safety of his second story window. And so he lay on his bed awaiting her return, looking at comic books to pass the time.

It was less than an hour later when he heard the "clip, clop" coming from the opposite direction. He carefully hid behind his pillow and peeked out the window; his heart beat faster and faster as the old woman got closer and closer to his house.

At that very moment, Mrs. Dexter walked silently into his bedroom with clean clothes and said in her cheery voice, "Whatcha lookin' at?"

Kyle was not cheered by his mother's unannounced greeting; instead, he pressed himself against the bedroom wall in sheer terror, wondering how the Hooting Woman had crept up behind him without his notice.

Discovering it was only his mother, Kyle relaxed and whispered, "Come here." His mother sat on Ricky's bed and followed Kyle's gaze out the window. The Hooting Woman performed as if she had rehearsed the scene a dozen times. She stopped directly in front of the Dexter house, bent forward and hooted two loud hoots. She moved on, dragging her bag of groceries beside her.

Kyle looked at his mother with raised eyebrows and wide eyes, waiting for her to explain. "Well, that's a first," was all she could think to say. But as she was leaving, she thought of something more. "You children will NOT give that woman any kind of grief or make fun of her in any way, do you understand?" Kyle nodded, surprised to hear his mother speak so forcefully and impressed by the starch in her tone. The Hooting Woman would be left alone.

Even though she was left alone, the Hooting Woman was often the topic of conversation during Dexter family meals.

"I saw Hoot, Hoot today," someone would begin.

"I wonder where she goes every day and what she carries in her bag."

"She lives two houses from Janette; it's on Logansport Street but it's a real shack."

The Hooting Woman was a mystery and a fascination and would remain so until later that month.

The leaves that had fallen so beautifully that one Saturday were now piled up in Kyle's front yard. The time had arrived for raking and hauling and burning them, and Kyle was given the honor.

And it *was* an honor to burn the leaves. It might be actual work to rake and haul the leaves to the back yard, but the excitement of putting a match to the dry pile was worth it all. Kyle had a touch of the pyromaniac in him and never lost the thrill of watching a match miraculously burst into flame, of seeing the tiny flame spread from one leaf to the next until the entire mountain of leaves was ablaze.

And from then on it was a race of Kyle's own creation. Before the flames could die away, Kyle had to hurry back to the front yard, fill the huge cardboard box with leaves and drag it back to the already dying fire. Kyle liked to tell himself that he had arrived too late, that he had just used the only match left in the entire world, that the eternal flame had died out and his people would be relegated to a life of cold and darkness from that moment on. But each time he poured the box of leaves onto the smoking ashes, it was the same.

At first, small whispers of smoke, one or two at the most, would snake their way through the leaves. Then more enthusiastic swirls would appear, and finally, billows of thick, white smoke that almost hid the pile from view. And then it happened. The entire pile would burst into one enormous yellow flame, and the race for more leaves would start all over again.

As Kyle topped off the box of leaves and started to drag it to the back yard, he heard a distinct and now familiar hoot and saw the Hooting Woman turn the corner onto Park Street and head his way. Kyle thought this would be a great time to take a bathroom break and was heading for the house when the Hooting Woman stopped several houses away. But instead of the abbreviated and slightly amusing hoot that she usually gave, this time, she bent at the waist and emitted a horrifying, elongated variation on the theme.

That single sound transformed the day from a place of innocent delight to a place of frightening reality. There was something dreadful in her cry, something that effectively unsettled Kyle's neatly predictable world and left it in ruins. In spite of the coolness of the day, Kyle realized that he was covered in sweat.

He ran for the house to find his mother. Mrs. Dexter was washing dishes but stopped mid-swish when she saw Kyle's concerned look. "What's wrong, sweetheart?"

"Can you come with me for a second?" he said. Kyle led the way to the front porch. Together they stood on the front steps, Kyle rocking nervously from side to side, his mother calmly drying her hands on a dishtowel.

The Hooting Woman passed the Dexter house without a sound, but just when Kyle thought nothing would happen, she stopped and cried out with the same dreadful, hair-raising wail as before. His skin crawled and he shivered uncontrollably.

"I need you to come with me, Kyle." Mrs. Dexter finished drying her hands, uncharacteristically tossed the dishtowel on the front steps, and the pair followed the Hooting Woman down Park Street.

Kyle glanced at his mother as they walked. There was something strong and brave about her demeanor, something in the tilt of her head and the firmness of her jaw that made Kyle glad they were on the same side.

The little woman shuffled down Logansport Street and up the sidewalk to her house, painfully made her way up three concrete steps and through the well-worn screen door to her home.

Kyle and his mother stood on the sidewalk and surveyed the scene before them. In the middle of a row of inviting, neatly painted and carefully manicured middle-class houses was a shack of startling contrast.

Enormous leaves of dried paint were tentatively clinging to the exposed wood. The roof of the small shack had a precarious lean to it and dozens of shingles were missing. The boards of the front porch were warped, and a piece of plywood had been placed over a gaping hole there. The screen door was suspended by one of its two hinges, and the screen itself was so torn that the flies and mosquitoes were hardly discouraged from entering.

How had he never really seen the house before? How had he walked down Logansport scores of times and never paused to wonder who lived in such dire conditions?

Mrs. Dexter opened her hand and Kyle slipped his into the familiar place. Each giving the other courage, the two crusaders walked into the unknown.

A knock on the screen door; some shuffling movements inside and finally, a second small, grey-haired woman peeked around the corner. Mrs. Dexter introduced herself and asked if she could come in. The woman thought and hesitated and finally, without a word, pushed the dilapidated screen door open; Kyle and his mother walked in.

When he took his first breath inside the house, Kyle felt as if he had been slapped in the face by the stench. The smell of rot and sweat and stale urine convinced Kyle that he would shortly be seeing his breakfast again. He almost screwed up his face in disgust, but the tight squeeze on his hand reminded him that he was in someone else's home. With each step, Kyle felt the rotting floor sag beneath the filthy shag carpet; it was as if he was sinking deeper and deeper into a dirty and frightening place.

Kyle, who knew comfort and warmth and peace in his own home, felt no comfort at all in the darkened room. It was inconceivable to him that people actually lived in such a place.

A few quiet words were exchanged between the second grey-haired lady and Mrs. Dexter. "Wait for me here," Mrs. Dexter said, pointing to a rocking chair that stood beside the front door. Kyle sat and began to carefully take in his surroundings.

He could see the entire house from his vantage point. To his left was a small bedroom. A mattress and a rumpled blanket on the floor and two cardboard boxes filled with clothes against the wall were its only furnishings.

In the front room in which he sat, there was a rocking chair, a space heater, and a filthy couch on which a pillow and blanket were stacked. It was clearly the second bed for the tiny house.

Straight back was the kitchen in which Mrs. Dexter and the second lady were sitting. And behind that was a back room in which the Hooting Woman was perched, birdlike, in a second rocking chair. She held tightly to the arms of the chair and vigorously rocked, head down and leaning forward to exaggerate her efforts even more. She might have been able to hear the kitchen conversation if she had chosen to, but her expression revealed a lonely remoteness, a great distance between her thoughts and her surroundings.

But by far the most disturbing aspect of the house was visible behind the rocking woman. One entire section of the back wall was missing! Kyle could see the trees and shrubs behind the house through the opening, easily large enough to walk through, and he could see thick green vines covering much of the wall of the room in which the Hooting Woman sat.

For the briefest of moments, Kyle, who had recently seen Disney's *Swiss Family Robinson*, was envious of living in a house without walls, in a house so close to nature and the outside world. But then stark reality shredded his naïve illusion with visions of summer heat, soaking rains, freezing winter nights, flies and wasps and mosquitoes and roaches and rats. He shivered at the thought of trying to sleep in such a house.

The two ladies talked and the third one rocked and Kyle slipped deeper and deeper into a dark depression. What would it be like to live in such a place every day? Mercifully the conversation ended and Mrs. Dexter took Kyle's hand again and began the walk home.

It was like Heaven to be out of that house. Kyle thought that nothing had ever seemed so bright and clean and beautiful as he looked at the clear blue sky above him. And nothing had ever smelt sweeter than the cool breeze that brushed his face on this particular fall morning.

Mrs. Dexter walked in silence. When Kyle glanced at his mother, he noticed that she was silently crying.

"What's wrong with little Hoot, Hoot?" Kyle asked.

"Her name is Agnes," she said with no condemnation in her voice. "And her sister is Maggie. It seems Agnes has stomach cancer. That's the reason she hoots. She thinks that if she makes a noise, the pain will go away."

They walked a bit further and Mrs. Dexter spoke again. "Something has to be done for those ladies." Her voice was choked with emotion. "Something has got to be done!"

As they walked in silence, Kyle knew that there was a conviction growing inside his mother, a conviction and a determination that would not be denied.

MRS. DEXTER'S CAUSE

It was Sunday night. The evening service for First Christian Church had ended and everyone had left for home except the ten members of the church board. Once a month the group stayed late to discuss church matters and make any decisions that needed to be made, from the mundane to the momentous, from deciding the ideal temperature for baptismal water to spending time in prayer for much-loved members of the congregation.

The ten had paid their dues before they reached the place of such responsibility. Each had been active in the church for years. Each was a respected family member, and each was known and respected in the community. They were bankers, business owners, doctors, lawyers, university professors and one more thing – each was a man.

That simple fact had made Vennie Dexter's request a unique and frightening one. She wished to address the board. No board member could remember a woman ever being at their meetings; in fact, none could remember a woman ever *wanting* to be at their meetings.

But the request had been made. The week before, Mrs. Dexter had written to each of the board members with her request. When they briefly gathered after the morning service and asked Pastor Dexter about the request, all he could say was, "She's a stubborn woman, gentlemen, but she's no loose cannon. I think we need to at least hear what she has to say."

They agreed, and that evening at 8:00 in the fellowship hall, a historic moment in the life of First Christian Church occurred – a woman was present for the regular meeting of the church board.

Four tables had been placed together with 12 chairs around the outside – ten for board members and two for Pastor and Mrs. Dexter. The coffee had been brewed and was flowing freely, and several of the men had already lit up in preparation for the meeting's start. Four smoked cigarettes, one a very pungent cigar and one an aromatic pipe.

The pipe smoker was Mr. Patterson, the gray head of the group and the chairman for that particular year. Vennie Dexter's father smoked a pipe and she had convinced herself that Mr. Patterson, because he was a pipe smoker, would have the same common sense and tender heart that characterized her father. She, therefore, determined to direct her comments for the evening to the gentleman with the pipe.

At precisely 8:00 an opening prayer was offered; then the minutes from the last meeting were read and approved, and the meeting was officially open for new business. Mr. Patterson took a draw on his pipe before he spoke.

"I understand from those who have been here even longer than I have, that this is a meeting of historic import. For the first time in our church history, we have at a church board meeting a woman present. And I believe I speak for all of us when I say that of all the women I could think of for this historic honor, Vennie Dexter would be my number one choice. And gentlemen, I would appreciate it if you would not tell my wife that I said so." There were chuckles all round.

"Now Vennie, I'm assuming you would like to get home and make sure the kids are ready for school tomorrow, so I will let your request to speak be item number one on our agenda tonight." He gently tamped down the hot tobacco in his pipe with his calloused fingertip, smiled at Mrs. Dexter and nodded for her to begin.

Mrs. Dexter unfolded the piece of paper she had taken from Kyle's Big Chief Tablet and began to summarize her thoughts. "First of all, gentlemen, thank you for this opportunity to address the board. I will attempt to be brief and to the point."

"Which would also make your presentation unique in the history of our board meetings," Mr. Patterson quipped. Everyone laughed at the truth behind the witticism. "I'm sorry, Vennie; please proceed."

Mrs. Dexter smiled and continued. "It was only six weeks ago that our Sunday School lesson dealt with Jesus' conversation with a young lawyer. When Jesus told him to love God and his neighbor, the young lawyer asked, 'And who is my neighbor?' Jesus answered the question with the familiar parable of the Good Samaritan. In telling the story, He basically said that our neighbor is anyone who has needs that we are aware of and able to meet."

At this point, she took a sip from the small glass of water that Pastor Dexter had placed on the table for her. Mr. Patterson smiled and nodded and Vennie Dexter continued.

"I have all confidence that each of you gentlemen would render compassionate aid and financial assistance to anyone who lay dying on Park Street. Am I right?"

Most of the men were caught off guard. They had no idea they were going to be asked to participate in Mrs. Dexter's presentation. Each nodded or mumbled affirmatively to acknowledge that they would assist a dying person on Park Street. Their strong suspicion that nobody ever would be dying on Park

Street made it much easier for them to answer in the affirmative.

At this point, each determined to pay closer attention to what Mrs. Dexter was saying since she might ask another question at any time.

"Well gentlemen, the person dying within a stone's throw from our church is not on Park Street, but on Logansport Street; but I am confident that the address does not change your commitment to help."

At this point in her presentation, Vennie told the story of Agnes and Maggie, of their dire physical circumstances, of Agnes's cancer and of their immediate need for help before winter showed up in earnest.

"I bring this to your attention because it seems to me that this is what the church is called to do. These ladies are literally our neighbors, and they desperately need our help."

The picture had been beautifully painted and vividly laid out for the board's consideration. Mr. Patterson drew on his pipe and the tobacco glowed even as his eyes glowed with appreciation. "Thank you, Vennie; let me assure you that we will discuss your concerns and that Don will let you know tonight of our conclusions."

Mrs. Dexter, her presentation complete, rose to leave, and every man around the table rose with her, several offering words of appreciation for her remarks and her courage.

When she was out of earshot, Mr. Patterson opened the meeting for comments. "Gentlemen, your thoughts."

Member #1 had a suggestion. "Our Sunday School offerings go to missions; we could designate these ladies as a local mission and use one of our Sunday School offerings to help them."

Mr. Patterson asked for clarification. "Don, what was our Sunday School offering this morning?"

"A little less than $100."

"I'm not sure that would make much of a difference for the ladies."

Member #2 spoke up.

"I don't mean to sound heartless [*a clear indicator that he was about to do precisely that*] but these ladies have lived through winter before under the same circumstances. It sounds to me like they are fairly used to how they're living. Sounds to me like they're from tough, pioneer stock who don't really mind a little brisk, fresh air."

Some were embarrassed by the statement; others were in shock that it was even voiced.

"Seems to me we have the means to bring these ladies into the 20th Century," Member #3 countered. "Chuck runs the lumber yard – I'll bet he could arrange for us to get the lumber at cost."

"I'd make sure it was donated," Chuck replied. "They owe me big time over there."

"And we have twenty men who know how to shingle a roof and throw up sheetrock and insulation and replace rotten boards and install carpet." Member #3 was getting excited. "New plumbing might take a weekend to pull off, but we could turn that shack into a home if we put our minds to it!"

Mr. Patterson and others were nodding in excited affirmation when Member #4 sprayed water on the growing flames of enthusiasm.

"A few observations, gentlemen. First of all, my heart goes out to these ladies, but keep in mind that they are not members of our church nor are any of their relatives. Secondly, they have not asked for our help. True, Vennie found them, but do you know how many people I could find that need help within a mile of our church? Can we help them all? Of course not. Do I wish we could? Of course I do. But you know the old saying: If 'ifs' and 'buts' were candy and nuts, oh, what a merry Christmas we'd have."

"I'm just asking you to be reasonable, gentlemen. We're a relatively small church and we can only do a few things. Do you realize what will happen when word gets out about what we've done? And don't think it won't! People who have never darkened the doors of our church will start showing up looking to have *their* roof replaced or *their* front porch fixed or *their* fixtures installed. As much as I'd like to help these ladies, we need to realize that while this one specific need might not sound like much, it's just like Pandora's Dam, and the little Dutch boy has his finger in it for now, but if he pulls it out..." Unable to continue his rapidly disintegrating analogy, Member #4 lifted his hands as if to say, "I think that says it all."

Since water was being tossed on the fire, Member #5 added a gallon or so. "I know no one wants to be the one to say this, but I also know we're all thinking it, so I might as well say it for everyone. What if God wants those ladies to be in the cold? What if they have lived lives of sin so that God's punishment, this poverty and this cancer, is falling upon them now? I mean, we might be interfering with the will of God if we make them comfortable."

There was such a silence when Member #5 concluded, that you could hear the tobacco burning as Member #9 took a puff on his cigarette.

Mr. Patterson, looking for some perspective, made a request. "Don, can you give us some insight into how the Judgment of God works? Now we've already had two sermons today, so just a short devotional, please." Hearty laughter followed with several *Amens*.

Donald Dexter gathered his thoughts and began. "The story of the Good Samaritan is as good a place to start as any. The man in need and the man rendering aid were not of the same religion; they were not even of the same race." He let those words sit for a moment and bring up uncomfortable pictures of a modern analogy. "There was no determination of the injured man's worthiness for help; there was no question raised about whether or not he deserved to be beaten up. Aid was simply rendered. And it cost the Samaritan; it cost him time and effort and money and potential embarrassment. Loving your neighbor it seems, will always cost us something."

"And as far as God giving us what we deserve? I don't know about you gentlemen," his eyes met and rested briefly on each one in the circle, "but I speak for myself. If God gave me what I deserved, I wouldn't be alive today. I wouldn't be the husband of a fine wife, the father of three delightful children, the pastor of a loving church and the friend of such fine men as you. That I am not dead or in Hell is what the Bible calls Mercy; that I am abundantly blessed with what I could never deserve is what the Bible calls Grace. And we, gentlemen, as God's people, are called to dispense both those qualities in His name."

Pastor Dexter rose to his feet and continued. "Gentlemen, since it was my wife who brought this concern to your attention, and since you might not feel free to speak your minds for fear of offending one of us, I am, with your permission, going to retire for the evening. Thank you for your service to this church, and," looking at Mr. Patterson, "I will await your call when you have reached a decision. Don't worry about how late it is; I'll be up."

He was almost to the door when an additional thought occurred to him. "One more thing. It has been suggested tonight that we should carefully consider our actions lest we be taken advantage of, lest we be overwhelmed with requests for assistance. I guess that could happen. In fact, we just might get 'assisted' right out of existence. But I don't think so."

"Maybe something entirely different will happen, something that none of us has envisioned. What if our actions are not only noted by people in need but are also noted by the people of God? What if church families all over Nacogdoches stand up ready to help people in their neighborhood, and their actions cause other churches to stand as well? Who knows, it just might be that our little, localized act of kindness could be the spark that sets this entire community on fire for God. I guess that's one more thought we ought to throw into the mix. Good night, gentlemen."

Pastor Dexter told his wife what he had said and done. He reported on some of the meeting, leaving out all the names and most of the discouraging comments. "We'll just have to wait and pray," he said.

It was past 11:00 when the phone finally rang. Pastor Dexter answered and listened for the longest time. "And goodnight to you, too," he said and hung up.

When he turned around, Vennie was there. "Well?" she said.

"They've decided to do all that you've suggested. The only reason the meeting took so long was all the talk about how to implement the plan. The ladies will be warm when the next cold front hits. They're starting on the work tomorrow morning."

Vennie placed her hand over her mouth and squealed like a teenager. "Oh, Don," is all she could manage to say.

Just the month before, the couple had gone to a presentation on the SFA campus of Robert Bolt's play, *A Man for All Seasons*. There was one line from the play that Donald Dexter had taken to heart for such a moment as this. Holding his courageous wife at arm's length and looking into her pretty, tear-filled eyes, he quoted the cherished line. "Why, it is a lion I married. A lion, a lion!"

Vennie melted into his embrace in grateful tears.

DECEMBER

GOD COUNTING

It was December 12th, only two weeks before Christmas and just a few days before school would be out for the term. Ninety-nine students out of a hundred were light-hearted and unencumbered, frolicking merrily toward their Christmas break. Kyle was the one-in-a-hundred who was not.

It had all started a few months back with an innocent visit to the family dentist. Kyle had opened wide and heard the great news that he had no cavities. But then life took a calamitous turn for the worse. The dentist had turned aside and spoken in serious, hushed tones to Mrs. Dexter.

He had basically told her that Kyle had lots of big, healthy teeth but not enough big, healthy jaw to accommodate them all. Things would get tight and messy in just a few years.

Did she want to plan for braces in Kyle's future, or did she want him to pull four of Kyle's permanent teeth now so that those remaining would be straight and true and not face a lifetime of pushing and shoving?

For Mrs. Dexter, who was already in the middle of dealing with and paying for Donna's braces, it was an easy decision. She chose the four extractions.

Ever since that day in October, there had been a lingering uncertainty about life for Kyle, an ominous whispering in the periphery of his subconscious, warning him not to enjoy life too much, not to be too carefree. All it took was one word to bring Kyle crashing back to reality, back to thoughts of his bleak future. And that one word was "extraction."

That was the word the dentist had used, and Kyle knew that it basically meant "to rip out by the roots." And Kyle was painfully, traumatically familiar with the concept.

He was six when his first loose tooth became an object of fascination in his life. With his tongue, he wiggled it non-stop throughout the day, for his own amusement and to the delight of those around him. He should have reserved the diversion of tooth-wiggling to the privacy of his own room, but he was a novice at such matters and as such, carried the delightful pastime a bit too far.

He was in the middle of a tooth-wiggling performance for Donna and Ricky when Mr. Dexter reached the end of his tooth-wiggling rope. "Come here, Kyle," he said as he took a handkerchief from his dresser drawer. "Let's see that tooth."

It all happened so fast! If his father had told him that he intended to pull his tooth, Kyle could have pleaded his case or burst into tears or reasoned that he had to go to the bathroom really bad.

But it was over in a heartbeat. Mr. Dexter put the handkerchief over the tooth, gripped it tightly, twisted and pulled and that was that. For Mr. Dexter, that was that; but not for Kyle, who let out a yelp of pain and topped it off with wave after wave of heart-breaking sobs.

Mr. Dexter had been a Depression-era farm boy, and as such he was not impressed. Among other hard times and difficult experiences, he had watched his mother sew up his own cut-open foot with her sewing needle and thread. Mr. Dexter, who as a teenager had been shot down over Italy and interred in a German POW camp for 18 months, was not moved. "That's enough, Kyle; it couldn't have hurt that much."

It was then that Mrs. Dexter picked up the handkerchief to retrieve Kyle's first tooth-fairy trophy and made a grievous discovery: there were two teeth in the handkerchief instead of one! Not only had Mr. Dexter's big fingers pulled out Kyle's obnoxious wiggler, but they had also extracted, ripped out by the roots, its very stable "I'm-planning-on-being-around-for-six-months-or-so" neighbor.

The going rate for tooth-fairy reimbursements in the Dexter home was twenty-five cents per tooth. Kyle put both teeth under his pillow that night and the tooth fairy, making partial restitution for past injuries, left a shiny silver dollar.

Yes, Kyle knew all about extractions; so he began to dread the coming day weeks before it arrived.

Finally, the Day of Multiple Extractions dawned. It was December-dark, cloudy and sinisterly gloomy. Kyle's un-tasted breakfast set like lead in his stomach and his internal butterfly activity was approaching maximum rowdiness.

The whole day was unnatural. Ricky and Donna were at school and Kyle wished with all his might that he could be there as well. Being home on a school day usually meant fever and chicken-noodle soup and *I Love Lucy* reruns. But not this day.

The cheerful Christmas candles and the Christmas tree lights burned with seasonal gaiety, apparently indifferent to Kyle's imminent doom. His mother had cut out the latest in a Christmas serial from *The Dallas Morning News* about one of Santa's elves, but the story was powerless to take Kyle's mind from the impending hour of horror that lay ahead.

It was time. A brief ride downtown, a trip up a dark flight of wooden steps, and Kyle and his mother were sitting on cold metal chairs in a strange smelling waiting room. Kyle's overactive imagination had erected impediment after impediment to the consummation of this unmentionable deed, but none of them had materialized.

Maybe the car wouldn't start. It did. Maybe the dentist would have a flat. He didn't. Maybe he would run out of Novocain. He had a fresh supply. Maybe the Russians would drop the bomb. They were uncharacteristically civilized on that bleak mid-winter day.

A lady in white escorted Kyle to the torture chamber and covered him with a large, thick white bib to keep the blood from staining his clothes. She left Kyle alone as his mom and the dentist continued their conversation in the outer room.

And then he saw it. A stainless steel tray on which was carefully placed a neat row of syringes filled with Novocain. Equally as ominous was the glistening pair of pliers (what else could you call them?) that lay beside them.

No subtlety here! No pretense that what lay ahead was going to be anything except a doling out of excruciating pain.

His mother sat in a chair against the wall; the dentist took his place beside Kyle and lifted the first shiny metal syringe in front of Kyle's ever widening eyes.

After some trite comment that was transparently designed (even to a fourth grader) to reassure him that this was not, after all, anything but an everyday occurrence, the dentist poised the needle and said, "Open wide."

Seeing no possible alternative before him, Kyle closed his eyes and did as he was told. The needle began to do its painful work and Kyle's mother, inexplicably, began to count.

"One, two, three, four…eighteen, nineteen, twenty." The first injection was over.

"Once more," the dentist said, and again Kyle scrunched up his eyes, dug his fingers into the vinyl chair and opened his mouth.

"One, two, three…" the count began again and somewhere in the lower twenties, it ended.

Four times that morning Kyle dug his fingers into the dentist's chair and four times his mother counted as the needle painfully prepared him for what was to follow.

Exhausted and numbed, the extractions were almost an afterthought in the whole process. And he made it, as his mother knew he would; he didn't die after all.

Even with a mouth full of gauze, Kyle's eyes closed the instant his head hit his pillow at home. In an hour he woke as his face began to tingle and itch.

As he lay in his bed, he thought back on the morning and was overwhelmed by his mother's wisdom. How had she known how to do what she did? How did she know that by simply counting she could transform what seemed unending and unbearable into something that was, in reality, brief and endurable?

Kyle closed his eyes and felt as fully as he could the deliciousness of the moment. It was over; IT WAS OVER! School would end soon and Christmas would follow soon after. And he was alive once more to greet such days and heartily embrace them.

Overwhelmed by exhaustion Kyle slept the sleep of the victorious warrior. Even as he drifted into oblivion, he had the familiar, unsettling feeling that he had once again encountered something that meant something else, something more. For years it would elude him.

But as the years passed, whenever those moments came when pain seemed unendurable and without end, whenever he was overwhelmed with a grief that seemed to extend forever into the future, Kyle remembered that frightening morning and the lesson learned in the dentist's chair, and he knew with reassuring certainty that Someone strong and good was very near, and that He was counting.

THE CHRISTMAS DANCE

ON YOUR MARK!

Nadine Davis missed the glory days of her collegiate experience. During her four years as an SFA Lumberjack, Nadine had twice represented her sorority in the homecoming parade, each time riding high on the back seat of a Cadillac convertible. She had also been a football sweetheart her senior year, jewels on her head and ermine on her shoulders at the 50-yard line.

And for four years she was a twirler in the SFA band. In her last year, Nadine was named "feature twirler". Her picture was on the front of every football program, and during the halftime of the two night games, the tips of Nadine's baton were ignited, the stadium lights were dimmed and she performed her flaming twirling routine to the rhythm of the SFA band and accompanied by the "oohs" and "aahs" of the appreciative crowd.

Such glory, once enjoyed, is hard to live without.

The glory had lingered a month or two more during the summer following her graduation. The entire campus and most of the community talked of Nadine's wedding, calling it the grandest Nacogdoches had ever seen.

The ancient, majestic pines bowed and scraped before the homecoming queen as she took her Pan-Hellenic beau's hand in marriage. Ron was flanked by eight fraternity brethren and Nadine by a giddy mixture of sorority sisters and fellow twirlers. A string ensemble played Bach and Mendelssohn; flashbulbs exploded in celebration over a hundred times as a Daily Sentinel photographer captured images of friends that would drift apart with the passing years. Corks were popped, gifts bestowed, and pledges of everlasting friendship exchanged.

But the glorious wedding came to an end, and the honeymoon as well was soon only a memory book filled with luggage tags, boarding passes, hotel receipts and postcards from half-dozen tropical ports of call.

Early that next fall, the doctor confirmed Nadine's suspicion that she was pregnant. Barely a year after her graduation, she was resting peacefully in a second-floor room of Memorial Hospital with her new daughter in her arms.

Nadine and Ron agreed to call their firstborn, Glinda.

In reality, Nadine chose the name and Ron simply acquiesced. When asked why the name "Glinda", Nadine had replied, "One of my childhood friends was named Glinda; I've always loved the name."

Actually, Nadine had never had a friend named Glinda, but she was a huge fan of the movie, *The Wizard of Oz,* and her favorite character was Glinda, the Good Witch of the South. When Nadine first saw Glinda on the silver screen, she saw in her someone who possessed all the qualities of ideal womanhood: beauty, grace, fashion, a crown and a magic wand. Nadine had enjoyed all of those, her baton acting as a suitable substitute for the magic wand.

And when Glinda was born, Nadine was determined that her daughter's life would be equally blessed with goodness and smiles, glitter and chiffon, honors and applause.

One September afternoon in 1960, Nadine was watching *American Bandstand,* waiting for Glinda to come home from school when the idea occurred to her. A dance! A dance for Glinda and all the other sixth graders at Raguet Elementary! It would be the perfect opportunity for Glinda to make her grand entrance into the stratospheric realm of Nacogdoches high society.

Oh, sure, the other girls would look nice, but Glinda would sparkle, a diamond among rhinestones. Nadine imagined how the other girls would hover around her little princess, admiring her hair, her jewelry, her Neiman Marcus dress, her sparkling shoes.

Nadine quivered with excitement as she envisioned her daughter's social coronation. And once again, the glory that had been hers, that had been quietly smoldering in her soul for over a decade, began to slowly warm and softly glow. Nadine knew it! Her glory would burn brightly once again, but this time, Glinda would bear the glorious flame on her behalf.

When it came to transforming her dream into reality, Nadine was an irresistible force, at times moving with the steady patience of a glacier, at other times with the explosive urgency of a volcano. But step by step, around some obstacles and directly over others, the dream moved toward reality.

A cup of coffee with a few carefully chosen moms; a subtle comment to Ron about how much more mature the young people were these days; some flowers and candy to Glinda's teacher along with a card that read, "When a simple 'thank you' is not enough"; and finally an "impromptu" remark at a PTA meeting that began, "This just came to me; I was wondering if we could…"

It was late one Saturday evening, just before Halloween, when Nadine finished her umpteenth phone call and slipped the receiver into its cradle. The realization caught her completely by surprise. It was finished! There were no more hurdles to clear! The dance was going to happen!

During the first week of November, the gold embossed invitations were sent out to every 4th, 5th and 6th grader at Raguet Elementary. The 4th and 5th graders were included for two reasons. First, there were simply not enough 6th graders at Raguet to constitute the grand ball that Nadine envisioned. And secondly, some of the 4th and 5th grade mothers were embarrassingly pushy, determined to have their daughters compete with Glinda for the unofficial title of Belle of the Ball. Nadine was not resentful; in fact, she welcomed the competition. The more rhinestones that surrounded Glinda, the more clearly her little diamond would stand out.

With the invitations in the mail, the rigorous planning stage was officially over and Nadine was finally free to dream. As she closed her eyes that cold November night, Nadine caught a glimpse of a fairy tale ending for Glinda's first dance. And every night after that, she would add another glimmering detail until the fantasy was complete.

It was the final dance of the evening. The turning, mirrored ball over the dance floor was sprinkling the room with multi-colored petals of light. The record began to play; it was Percy Faith's "Theme from A Summer Place". The dance floor was empty except for Glinda and some nameless, strikingly handsome young boy. Everyone encircled the dancing pair and looked on admiringly. And Glinda laid her head against her prince's shoulder, closed her eyes and smiled. And Nadine's eyes closed as well, and as she slept, she smiled.

Kyle and Donna burst through the front door in unison, closed it behind them and ran to the space heater to warm their tingling fingers and faces. When they were sufficiently thawed from the cold, they began to address the problem that presented itself every afternoon after school. It was 3:00, they were hungry; and dinner was at 6:00. Snack time!

On this particular day, it would be "the regular."

"You do the peanut butter and I'll do the jelly," Donna said as she moved into the kitchen. Like two cogs in a well-oiled machine, Donna and Kyle fulfilled their appointed tasks. Donna covered ten crackers with grape jelly while Kyle smeared ten crackers with peanut butter. Then they shared their efforts with the other so that each had ten potential PB&J cracker sandwiches.

But in the Dexter home, there was one more ingredient. Donna put the jelly back in the refrigerator and took out the special ingredient that would distinguish the Dexter after-school snack from all others in Nacogdoches County. Kyle got two clean knives and gave one to Donna as she carefully unscrewed the lid from the mayonnaise jar. A touch of mayo was all it took to turn a traditional PB&J cracker sandwich into a tasty treat for the ages.

Their snack completed and their adolescent appetites appeased for the moment, Donna and Kyle put the ingredients away and washed off the silverware. Kyle was heading for the television set to keep his afternoon appointment with The Three Stooges when he heard Donna cry out from the living room: "We got letters!"

Kyle was used to getting a dollar in the mail from each grandmother on his birthday and a Christmas card from his Sunday school teacher each year, but anything beyond that was the stuff of mystery and suspense.

He and Donna opened their identical letters in unison and silently read the contents. "You are cordially invited", the gold letters proclaimed. It was all there: Christmas Dance; Sacred Heart Catholic Church Parish Hall; Saturday, December 17 at 7:30 p.m.; Semi-formal Dress.

"I don't believe it," Donna squealed; "my first dance!" She was up the stairs and in her closet in a flash, pushing everything that "just wouldn't do" to the left and putting her favorite, fanciest dresses on the far right. Kyle was in a hurry, too. *The Three Stooges* had already started.

Kyle was not worried about the dance. He had naturally assumed that "you are cordially invited" included the option of saying a simple "no thank you" and continuing your life as usual. He assumed it was like being offered a dish with raw onions in it. Mrs. Dexter had told Kyle to simply say "no thank you" without offering any commentary on how he hated onions or how he had actually thrown up in the middle of an El Chico restaurant when Mr. Dexter insisted that he eat the raw onions on his enchilada. Surely, Kyle thought, a simple, polite "no thank you" would be quite sufficient.

But since Mrs. Dexter was almost as excited as Donna that her little ones had been invited to their first dance and since Kyle almost certainly would not throw up if forced to attend, the "no thank you" option was soon no option at all.

"You'll need a haircut; we can do that next Saturday. And you'll need a new sports coat and slacks; you've almost grown out of the ones you're wearing now." The possibility of the dance was inevitably, incrementally becoming a reality for Kyle, and there was nothing he could do to stop the juggernaut of his mother's enthusiasm.

A good quarter of Kyle's class had the privilege of saying, "No thank you." The dance looked like a lot of work to their parents, so those lucky guys could stay home that Saturday night if they chose to, and they chose to!

Another quarter of the class came from families that considered dancing, along with comic books, top 40 radio, mixed swimming, and motion pictures, as just another snare of the Devil for the unsuspecting modern day young person. For those families, what they did NOT do was considered to be their main claim to godliness, and dancing was close to the top of the list of things to avoid. Their children would not be attending the Christmas dance!

There was a third quarter of the population that had no moral objection to their children attending a dance. They had a more relaxed, yet highly principled philosophy that could basically be summarized as, "You may go to the dance as long as you don't ask me to chaperone."

And there was the final quarter of Nacogdoches society, Don and Ven

Dexter among them, who were delighted that their children were invited to a dance and who would do all they could to see that they attended.

"Someone has worked long and hard on this dance, Kyle", his mother reminded him when he begged not to go, "and you are not going to hurt their feelings by staying home. So you might as well get used to the idea: you're going."

GET SET!

The dance was only a week away. Kyle and his father were spending a Saturday morning checking off the items on Mrs. Dexter's "still to do" list.

The haircut was the easy part. Kyle sat in the barber chair at the SFA Barber Shop and looked at his reflection. Mirrors on both sides of the room made his reflection, in reality, the reflection of a reflection of a reflection of a reflection until Kyle simply disappeared in a pin point of ever diminishing images of himself. Kyle found himself wishing he could ride the trail of those images into another world, a world that had never heard of dances. But it was not to be.

Mr. Lambert laid aside his scissors and turned the barber chair so that Kyle could see out the front window onto North Street and the reality of a cold, rainy December morning in Nacogdoches, Texas. There would be no escaping his fate. A quick dusting of his neck, a flurry of aromatic powder, and Kyle and his dad were on their way to find the perfect semi-formal attire for the big dance.

They tried the old reliable places, Beall Brothers and Mize Department Store, without any success. Nothing that was Kyle's size looked right, and everything that looked like it was made for a Christmas dance was too large. As Kyle and his dad drove for home, a glimmer of hope was kindled in Kyle's heart. He imagined his dad breaking the news to his mom.

"We tried everywhere, Vennie! There's just nothing out there that will fit the boy. It looks like he's going to have to stay home next Saturday night after all."

Kyle was mentally rehearsing his best "I'm just as disappointed about this as you are, Mom" look, when the light of hope faded. Just blocks from the safety of the Park Street driveway, Donald Dexter had a moment of insight. "Of course," he said. He slowed the car, looked in the rearview mirror, did a u-turn on Mound Street, and headed back toward the downtown area.

But when he got to Main Street, instead of turning right, where all the familiar stores were, he turned left. A few blocks later he pulled over and parked on the corner of Shawnee and Main.

"Archie's Tailor Shop" the sign said above the neat, new store. Kyle had never been there before. As they prepared to get out, Kyle noticed that there were several older men sitting in chairs on either side of the entrance. They were each Black. Kyle wondered if his dad knew what he was doing.

The bell above the door gave a loud ring as Kyle and his father walked in. The store looked a great deal like other clothing stores Kyle had visited: tables full of shirts, rows of suits and coats and slacks, and a wall of shoes. But there were differences as well, and Kyle had plenty of time to look around.

Most noticeably, the three young men who attended the store were Black. Each was dressed for Sunday morning in a beautiful suit with coordinated shirt and tie. And each responded the same way when Kyle and his dad made their entrance: they froze.

On each surprised face was written two obvious thoughts: This has never happened before, and What do I do now? In the uncomfortable, silent moments that followed, Kyle had all the time in the world to look around the store.

He noticed the scattered Christmas decorations and was captivated by a window display that featured statues of Santa and three very lively children who were running into his open arms. The display closely resembled one in Mrs. Hartsfield's window at school except for one significant difference: the three children AND the Santa were Black!

Kyle's mental picture of Santa Clause had always been based on the yearly Coca-Cola posters that featured the white-haired, rosy-cheeked, white-skinned Santa. He had never imagined Santa any other way. It was now becoming clear to Kyle that other children saw Santa through different eyes and thought of him in different lights.

If Kyle was a bit uncomfortable entering Archie's, he soon became enormously so. None of the young men who watched their entrance moved to give them any assistance. Even a fourth grader could tell that they were not welcome at Archie's.

Two of the young men whispered to each other and the older of the two approached the two white interlopers. Without a smile or a word of greeting the young man quietly said, "I think you may have come to the wrong store."

How would his father respond? What would he say, could he say? Kyle never got the chance to find out.

Before Mr. Dexter could reply, there was a flurry of movement, a scattering of personnel, and the appearance of a handsome, well-dressed, middle-aged black man. His eyes were wide with emotion and aglow with righteous anger. It was Archie, *the* Archie of Archie's Tailor Shop, and he was an avenging angel whose mission was to right a great wrong.

It was a little over a month before when Pastor Jeremiah Wilson had shared a story with his congregation.

"My son, Elijah, was stopped last night on his way home…"

The congregation had heard and felt every word.

"The officer was giving him a hard time, and I think you know why."

Each member of the congregation remembered other injustices they had experienced or heard about.

"A man stood in the gap for my son….a White man."

A handsome tenor in the church choir heard those words with amazement.

"Maybe, just maybe things are changing. When a White man stands up to another White man for the sake of a young Black man…well then maybe, just maybe things are changing."

Archie whispered a silent prayer that morning. "Lord, if you're bringing about a movement of change in this land, in this community, I would dearly love to be a part of it."

A month later, in front of a colorful display of shirts and ties, Archie got his chance.

"Don't you know who this is?" Archie had physically turned the young man so that their faces were only inches apart. As he hotly spoke his mind to his young apprentice, he pointed toward Pastor Dexter.

"This gentleman is a preacher of the Gospel and a man of God." If the young man he was addressing had a dozen questions at this point, Pastor Dexter had a dozen more. Archie knew who he was and what he did. How? Donald Dexter was almost certain he had never before met Archie; how then did Archie know so much about him?

Nacogdoches was a small town in more than just numbers. It had small town ways and a small-town personality. And one of the chief characteristics that makes a small town a small town is that everyone knows everyone else's business. Especially if that business was a bit spicy, or a tad tawdry, or contained just a smidgen of scandal.

When a popular cheerleader dropped out of school and went to spend a year with her aunt in Louisiana, the entire town knew the reason why. The "secret" was so thoroughly discussed that it might as well have been on the front page of *The Daily Sentinel*.

But there was another side to the gossip coin, a benevolent side, a small-town trait that made you proud to live in a small town. For as committed as the population of Nacogdoches was to spreading the juicy and the scandalous, it was just as committed to spreading the noble, the courageous and the decent.

When NHS quarterback Billy Ray Strickland gave up his collegiate football scholarship, the whole community knew why. When he drove to Louisiana and brought back his baby and his bride-to-be, the whole town silently cheered. And when he settled down in Nacogdoches with his new family and began to work at this father's feed store, he made every resident of Nacogdoches proud to live in a community where people still made the decent and the noble and the courageous choice.

And on prom night, when Pastor Dexter had made his courageous stand, the benevolent whisperings began as well. From son to father; from pastor to congregation; from neighbor to neighbor; the charitable gossip spread until everyone in the Black community was aware that they had a friend in Pastor Donald Dexter. And Archie Sutter, proprietor of Archie's Tailor Shop, was high on his list of admirers.

"If I'm not mistaken," Archie continued his remarks to the young clerk, "there are quite a few shirts in the back that need to be refolded, re-pinned and made ready for display. But before you take care of that little item, I would very much like for you to show me that you remember how it is that you are to greet *everyone* who enters my store." Archie strongly emphasized the word "everyone".

The young man swallowed, turned to Donald Dexter, and extended his hand. As Mr. Dexter took his hand, the young man shook it strongly and said as he had been taught, "I'm Steven; welcome to Archie's Tailor Shop."

"Thank you," Mr. Dexter replied and smiled. "It's good to be here."

When Steven had made his way to the back room, Archie smiled upon his most recent customers. "And now, how may I help you two gentlemen?"

Kyle's father explained about the Christmas dance and about his inability to find a suitable outfit for Kyle. Archie beamed a great smile at Kyle, looked him over with a tailor's keen eye and proclaimed, "Why, I think we can make this young man shine; yes sir, make him look like Sam Cooke when he's just about to walk on stage."

Archie must have seen the lack of recognition in Kyle's eyes at the mention of Sam Cooke. "You do know Sam Cooke, don't you?" he asked. Kyle looked at his dad for help, but Mr. Dexter simply smiled and raised his eyebrows as if to say, "You're on your own, buddy."

But Archie didn't let Kyle wonder for long. Right there in the middle of the entrance to Archie's Tailor Shop, Archie began to snap his fingers, then to rhythmically move his body, then softly to sing in a sweet, tenor voice, "That's the sound of the men, working on the chain gang; that's the sound of the men, working on the chain gang."

Kyle smiled and nodded at the familiar song. "Sam doesn't just sing like a prince," Archie said, "but he dresses like one as well. Let's see what we can do for you, Kyle."

Kyle, in his faded jeans, tennis shoes and SFA sweatshirt, looked to Archie like the Liza Doolittle of the haberdashery world. But Archie was his Henry Higgins, the skilled master who would turn the ragged young sow's ear into a silken purse before the first record played at the Christmas dance.

Archie whisked Kyle into a small room with mirrors on three sides. While his dad watched, he tried on coats and slacks and shirts in more varieties and materials and colors than he knew existed. Nothing fit the slight fourth grader well, but he was, after all, in Archie's Tailor Shop. Archie tucked and turned and chalked and pinned until he finally sighed and said, "Everything should be ready by Thursday."

Archie walked Kyle and his father to the front door, shook both their hands and smiled through the glass as they drove away.

"Have you been there before, Dad?"

"No; that was my first time, too."

"But he seemed to know you. How does Archie know you?"

"I have no idea, Kyle; I have no idea."

"And he seemed to like you, too."

Pastor Dexter remembered the gracious manner, the kind words, and the benevolent smile. "I have a feeling Archie likes just about everyone."

"Me too," Kyle said, and they rode in silence the rest of the way home.

It was Thursday evening, only forty-eight hours until the Christmas Dance. Kyle Dexter stood most uncomfortably in the center of the living room while his family inspected him from every direction. The gray slacks, rich blue sports coat, and snappy blue tie had transformed Kyle into a miniature Dick Clark. Archie had delivered the miracle he had promised.

"Kyle, you look so handsome," his mother gushed. "Any young girl would be honored to dance with you."

Donna was wearing the dress she had chosen for the big night. She stood beside Kyle and pleaded with Mr. Dexter. "Daddy, get a picture of Kyle and me, please."

Mr. Dexter touched the flash bulb to his tongue before he inserted it into the Kodak Brownie. "Cheese", said Donna and Kyle in unison, and the explosion of light captured the moment for posterity.

Weeks later, as the Dexters sat one evening looking at the latest family slides, the moment was relived. Everyone had the same thought as they looked at Kyle and Donna in their best clothes, but it was Ricky who said it: "Kyle looks like he's about to throw up!"

Everyone laughed, including Kyle. The camera often froze moments of time with hilarious results: eyes at half-mast, someone licking their lips in preparation for the shot, an all-too-transparent glare of disapproval or an overly zealous smile.

But the image captured by Donald Dexter's Kodak that Thursday evening was no trick of the camera; it was, in fact, an accurate representation of his son's spirit at that moment in time. Because it was at that precise moment, only forty-eight hours before the big dance, that Kyle Dexter came to a horrifying realization that no haircut could remedy, that no perfectly tailored wardrobe, even Archie's finest, could assuage: Kyle Dexter had realized for the first time that he did not know how to dance!

How had he thought of everything else except the most obvious? It was, after all, a Christmas DANCE he was going to.

Kyle had watched a few episodes of American Bandstand and had witnessed the intricate choreography of the dancers. There was no way he could come close to learning those steps before Saturday night.

When he had changed back into his school clothes, Kyle moped into the kitchen for an evening snack. His mom, reading his body language, asked what was wrong.

"I don't know how to dance," Kyle blurted out, too dejected to hide his despair or try to lessen the severity of his predicament.

"Well, I guess it's time you learned." His mother dried off her hands and led the way into the living room. "Come on," she said, and went to the record cabinet for some suitable learn-to-dance music.

While Kyle did not know the first thing about dancing, his mother did! She had kicked up her heels to the Big Band sounds of the forties. She had moved with the best of the swing dancers to the tunes of Glenn Miller, Tommy Dorsey, and Benny Goodman. Kyle was in the hands of an expert.

Mrs. Dexter put on a Johnny Mathis record, carefully lowered the needle to play "Chances Are" and waited for the music to begin.

"The girls will most likely be sitting in chairs around the dance floor." Vennie sat on the couch and continued her instructions. "Walk up to one of the girls from your class, bow slightly and ask, 'May I have this dance?' When she says 'yes', take her hand and lead her to the dance floor."

Kyle stood before his mother and bowed, one hand on his stomach and the other behind his back, just like he had seen Tony Curtis bow in "The Black Shield of Falworth."

"Very nice, Kyle", his mother said.

"May I have this dance?" Kyle asked. Mrs. Dexter smiled, extended her hand, and Kyle led her to the middle of the living room.

"Now take my right hand in your left," they fumbled until their hands were together properly, "put your right hand on the small of my back and move to the music."

Kyle had no problem with the rhythm. Mrs. Rudisill, his music teacher at Raguet, had encouraged her younger students to beat time with rhythm sticks and march in circles to the beat of her thunderous piano. Kyle rocked back and forth in precise rhythmical response to the music until the song ended.

"Now, walk me back to my chair and say 'thank you very much'." After dancing through both sides of the Johnny Mathis album, Kyle was graduated with honors from the Vennie Dexter School of Dance. In forty-eight short hours, his credentials would be put to the test.

GO!

In the blink of an eye, it was Saturday night and the final preparations for the dance were almost complete. Donna had dressed early and Mrs. Dexter had driven her to Janette's so that she and Janette could ride with their friends, Wendy and Becky, to the dance. Girls, Kyle learned that night at the dance, tend to travel in small flocks, not only to dances but to the restroom, to the punch bowl and anywhere else they might consider moving. Kyle, however, would be moving through the night completely on his own.

He gave his comb a few more opportunities to bring his hair to the point of perfection. He had used his dad's Brylcreem to make sure no hair was out of place. "A little dab'll do ya" was the Brylcreem slogan, but Kyle had used two generous dabs for insurance. No sense in risking an uprising on this special night. Tonight, every hair would behave!

Kyle shifted the comb in his hand, moved it to his forehead and with one practiced motion, flipped his short bangs so that they stood up smartly. And Kyle knew that with two dabs of Brylcreem, the flip would last all night.

His mother's voice called up the stairs. "It's seven-twenty; have you brushed your teeth?"

"Yes, ma'am," he called back. "I'll be down in a second."

Kyle eased the bathroom door closed, got out his toothbrush and loaded it with an extra glob of Ipana toothpaste. He quietly brushed, wiped his mouth and took one last look in the mirror.

He checked the hair, the face, and the clothes. All passed muster. Then he simply looked into the frightened blue eyes in the mirror. The butterfly activity in his stomach was constant and intense. Kyle took a deep breath and spoke to the trembling young man who was looking back at him. "What the heck are we doing?"

He turned out the bathroom light and made his way downstairs.

As Mrs. Dexter drove Kyle to the parish hall, she remembered her first dance. It had not gone well. Her mother had made Vennie's hair curl like Shirley Temple's, but her mother could do nothing to give her Shirley Temple's cute, chubby arms and legs. Vennie was as thin as a rail, and her long, thin legs were highlighted by the volume of petticoats beneath her dress. She sat the entire dance without dancing once and had never forgotten the humiliation of the night.

"Kyle," she started, carefully choosing her words, "you boys are lucky in one sense in that you get to dance as much as you want to. If you want to ask ten girls to dance, you can. If you just want to ask one girl to dance over and over, you can do that, too."

Vennie recalled the lonely chair at her first dance. "But we girls don't have it so lucky. We have to sit and wait…and hope that some young boy will ask us to dance. Otherwise…we just sit."

Mrs. Dexter, not wanting to hurry the conversation, pulled into the Piggly Wiggly parking lot across from the Catholic Church, turned off the engine and turned to face Kyle.

"There will be girls there tonight who are well-dressed and popular, and all the boys will be waiting in line to dance with them. And that's okay. But there will also be girls there tonight who are not wearing new dresses, who are not the popular ones that get picked first when you're playing games at recess."

The emotions of her first dance were coming back to Vennie Dexter. She struggled to keep her voice from quivering as she continued.

"They need to dance with a handsome boy like you, Kyle. They need to feel the honor and joy of being asked to dance by such a sweet boy." She took Kyle's hand in hers and gave it a squeeze. "Promise me you'll keep your eyes open for those girls."

Kyle nodded his understanding. In another moment he was opening the car door in front of the parish hall. "Have fun, Sweetheart; I'll be right here at ten-thirty."

Vennie watched her son walk the long sidewalk to the parish hall. She had never seen Kyle walk so slowly and so deliberately. He reminded her of Ronald Coleman walking to the guillotine in "A Tale of Two Cities." She smiled at the ridiculousness of the thought as she drove away. Kyle, however, was not smiling.

Nadine and Ron Davis stood just inside the door of the Sacred Heart Parish Hall. They smiled and shook the hand of each person who entered.

"Welcome to the dance; we hope you have a wonderful time. Welcome to the Christmas Dance; help yourself to punch and cookies."

After Kyle passed through the official greeting gauntlet, he noticed several uncomfortable differences between his dance lessons and the parish hall. First of all, it was a lot darker than it was in the Dexter living room; secondly, they weren't playing Johnny Mathis; and finally, none of the young ladies sitting in the chairs along the wall was his mother!

Kyle scanned the room and noticed that there was a group of guys standing together in the corner. As he approached them, he saw the reason for the congregation – a huge bowl of red fruit punch and half-a-dozen trays filled with enticing Christmas cookies. Like moths to a porch light they had swarmed to the object of their desire.

Kyle saw Benjie in the group, got a plate of cookies and joined him. As the two reflected upon the evening, Kyle considered for the first time that the night might not be a complete disaster.

The disc jockey welcomed everyone to the dance. He was a high school-aged guy that Kyle had seen on occasion when he waited for the bus on the high school campus. "All right everybody," he said in an excited voice, "it's time to do the latest, craziest dance. It's sweeping the nation, true; but tonight it's sweeping through the parish hall. LET'S TWIST!!!"

Kyle was surprised when almost everyone around him cheered and clapped. Many made their way to the dance floor as Chubby Checker drew them all into a twisting frenzy. Donna and her friends were twisting; even Benjie was twisting with his girlfriend, Betty. It didn't look that hard, but it was considerably different from the moves he had mastered at the Vennie Dexter School of Dance. He decided to stay behind and guard the punch and cookies while the majority twisted the night away.

Nadine had scripted the events of the evening to maximize her daughter's entrance. In the frenzy of preparations for the dance, Nadine had never forgotten her primary goal – to introduce Glinda into Nacogdoches society and to make the introduction a grand and memorable one.

Nadine and Glinda had driven to Dallas the weekend before and had been at the downtown Neiman-Marcus store when it opened at 9:00. Five hours later, with the car full of bags and boxes, they left for home.

"No one will outshine my baby at the dance," Nadine proclaimed to no one in particular as she drove. Glinda, who was too exhausted to be excited, slept all the way to Nacogdoches.

Nadine's instructions to Glinda on the night of the dance were extensive. "Now the girls are going to want to gather around you and look at your dress and your hair and your shoes. They may even want to touch your dress. That's okay; you can let them. And when they ask you where you got it, be sure to say you got it in Dallas at Neiman-Marcus. And do NOT mention that it was on sale. It is still an official Neiman-Marcus dress with a real Neiman-Marcus tag inside. And when the young boys ask you to dance, well, if you don't want to dance with one of them, just say, 'My dance card is filled for this dance.' Even if it's not, you are still allowed to say that. It's a completely acceptable practice at dances. It's done all the time. And do not let any of that red punch get even close to your dress! And don't eat any of those Christmas cookies; cookies just don't go with a Neiman-Marcus dress. You are free to eat all the cookies you want once you get home. Other than that…well, have a great time, Darling!"

The disc jockey had the script; Nadine held her breath and gave him the "thumbs up" sign.

When the record ended, the disc jockey read his lines. "I hope you're all having a wonderful time tonight, boys and girls. I guess by now, everyone has arrived. Wait a minute;…" Nadine wished he had practiced his lines more; there was no excitement or spontaneity in his voice. "Wait a minute; I believe I see a late arrival. Is that Glinda Davis? Let's all welcome Glinda to the Christmas Dance!"

As Glinda stepped through a side door, the speakers blared out "Let the Little Girl Dance". The mirrored ball over the dance floor exploded with light for the first time that night, and shards of color began to fly around the room. Nadine clapped wildly as she watched Glinda step into the room, but only a few others clapped with her. Nadine had completely underestimated the degree to which a mirrored ball could captivate a crowd's attention, especially a crowd that had never experienced the dancing lights before. What Nadine intended as a minor accessory to Glinda's grand entrance had become instead the center of everyone's attention.

Guys began to chase individual flecks of light around the room. A couple of sixth-grade boys lifted empty cookie trays and began to reflect the reflections. The splashing of light continued to fascinate the party crowd, and Glinda made her grand entrance almost completely unnoticed.

Nadine was crushed. "Haven't they ever seen lights before?" She spat out the words to Ron as she fought back the tears of disappointment.

Glinda, on the other hand, was just happy to be with her friends. She ran to the circle of sixth-grade girls and began to frolic with them in the dancing flecks of light. They held hands and danced in groups of three and four. No one cared where anyone else got their dress or how much it cost. Everyone was enjoying the Christmas Dance once more, only this time, Glinda was part of the crowd.

As the evening continued, Nadine was horrified when Glinda accepted cups of red punch from boys on two separate occasions, and she couldn't believe it when Glinda joined with the other girls in eating the large, iced Christmas cookies. And she was almost in tears when Glinda danced with "ordinary" boys. Nadine almost screamed for Glinda to use her "my-dance-card-is-filled-for-this-dance" option, but Glinda seemed only intent on enjoying herself, and she danced with everyone who asked her.

Nadine's fantasy had fallen flat: the grand entrance, the diamond among rhinestones, the Belle of the Ball, the romantic last dance. The fantasy had crumbled before her eyes, and as Nadine considered her shattered dream, she slipped into a great, despondent funk.

"Take me home, Ron; you can come back and pick up Glinda later."

"No," he said with a touch of anger in his voice, "you and I are the hosts of this dance and we're going to see the thing through to the end."

He had grown tired of hearing Nadine's plan over the past months. He had been embarrassed as she schemed to turn Glinda into some privileged Highland Park debutante. And he had grown angry when he finally understood that Nadine was using their daughter, *using her*, to relive her old glory days.

"And smile", he said, "Some guests are just arriving."

Kyle had palled around with Benjie for the majority of his time at the dance. The two of them had eaten more Christmas cookies than any other five boys at the dance, and Kyle's lips and tongue were bright red from all the fruit punch he had drunk.

At eight-thirty they had walked across the street to the Piggly Wiggly and looked through the comic books on the newsstand. That lasted a good twenty minutes until the impatient checker had asked the infamous "are you buying or just looking" question. Kyle had enough understanding about rhetorical questions to prevent him from replying, "We're just looking."

When they got back to the dance, Benjie and Kyle were feeling comfortable enough to try something daring. They moved to the far side of the refreshment table, pretended to drop something on the floor, and then, while hidden from view, they slipped beneath the table. Since the tablecloth came all the way to the floor, Kyle and Benjie were perfectly concealed and in a world of delightful isolation.

Kyle and Donna and Ricky often played "fort" on rainy days. A card table and a quilt were the only necessary ingredients for creating the fort. After that, the possibilities were as boundless as the Dexter imagination. With a pillow and blanket, a flashlight, a few comic books, and some vanilla wafers to nibble on, "fort" could easily fill an otherwise tedious rainy afternoon.

Kyle and Benjie sat cross-legged under the table in their Sunday best. The loud music allowed the boys to whisper without fear of discovery. But whenever toes appeared beneath the tablecloth, the whispering ended and the listening began.

On more than one occasion, conversations intended "for your ears only" were overheard by the two hidden eaves-droppers. Words spoken with tender affection caused the boys to roll to their backs with gut-tightening hilarity, especially when they could recognize the identity of the lovers. Fortunately, both boys were blessed with the ability to laugh silently.

After a while, the experience lost its newness and the boys reemerged without discovery. Benjie glanced at the clock on the wall, told Kyle that he'd see him at school on Monday and headed for the door. Kyle was alone.

It was nine-thirty, and the sixty minutes until Mrs. Dexter would pull to the curb stretched before Kyle like an eternity. He had successfully navigated through the first two hours of the dance without dancing once, but in every one of those moments, even the ones encrusted with sugar or punctuated with hilarity, his mother's words rang in his ears: "Promise me you'll keep your eyes open for those girls."

Subtly, secretly, Kyle had. And it was just as his mother had said. Most of the girls were asked to dance, some over and over, others a few times only. But there was a handful of girls who had only budged from their chairs to visit the restroom or the refreshment table. All but one were fifth or sixth graders and therefore socially out of Kyle's league. But one was from his class – Debbie.

The same Debbie whose smile and sparkling eyes had welcomed Kyle on his first day at Raguet. The same Debbie who had always touched Kyle's thumb when the class played "Seven-up". The same Debbie who had sought Kyle's attention and affection in a hundred ways over the past few years. The same Debbie who had been ignored and put off by the insensitive words and unkind actions of the once proud, but now disgraced, president of the Nacogdoches Chapter of Girl Haters Club, International. It was *that* Debbie that Fate, with a wry sense of humor, had determined would be Kyle's first dancing partner.

To Kyle, it seemed as if an entire universe of choices had been narrowed to one. If a red carpet had rolled from his feet to Debbie's or a flashing light had appeared above her head reading, "Available for Dancing", his course could not have been more obvious. Kyle understood perfectly. If he was to remain true to himself and true to his mother's wishes, he would ask Debbie to dance.

When the inevitability of the moment sank in, the butterflies in Kyle's stomach began to roughhouse in a most ungentlemanly manner. If the butterflies were moving at "battle speed" when Kyle walked into the parish hall, they had increased to "attack speed" when he decided he would ask Debbie to dance, and as he began to inch his way in her direction, his butterfly population reached "ramming speed."

Debbie noticed Kyle moving closer, but turned her head slightly to one side, pretending to look at the dancers instead. He had disappointed and hurt her in a hundred ways in the past, but her heart had miraculously not grown calloused from the regular pain of those disappointments. She hoped this might be the moment when Kyle Dexter finally returned her kindness and affection, but she kept that hope on a tight leash lest it run wild.

Kyle waited for the fast dance to end. Some of the dancers stayed on the dance floor; others returned to their seats. After a moment, the lights were lowered and the mirrored ball began to spin and shower the room with dancing flecks of light. It was as if the butterflies in Kyle's stomach had escaped and were continuing their escapades on the floor and walls of the parish hall.

Kyle knew that the lowered lights and the mirrored ball foretold the coming of a slow dance, the kind Kyle had been trained for at Vennie Dexter's School of Dance. This was his moment.

With his heart pounding in his ears and his stomach turning cartwheels, Kyle turned and began to cross the expanse that stretched between him and Debbie. As she saw him coming her way, Debbie's eyes locked with Kyle's and her lips were transformed into a sweet smile.

Kyle had only one line to get right: "May I have this dance?" But that was no reassurance to him. He also had only one line in the radio play his class had recorded in the third grade. He was to say, "Come in and tell me what I can do for you." Instead, when they passed the hot microphone to him, Kyle had panicked and said, "Come in and tell me what you can do for me." The class had giggled uncontrollably and Kyle had learned an important lesson: no matter how small the task before him might be, he was still quite capable of making an utter fool of himself.

Somehow he found himself standing before Debbie's chair. She was smiling up at him as he bowed slightly and asked, word perfect, "May I have this dance?" Thankfully, it was days later when it first occurred to Kyle that there were two answers to that question.

But for Debbie, there was only one answer. She smiled broadly and, Kyle realized for the first time, beautifully, and stood to join him on the dance floor.

Kyle took Debbie's sweaty hand in his sweaty hand, and then placed his right hand lightly on the small of her back. It was in the next moment that Kyle realized that Debbie had been trained in another school of dance. Instead of staying at a reputable distance, like his mother did, Debbie slipped close to Kyle, wonderfully close, so that he could smell her intoxicating fragrance and actually feel the warmth of her breath on his neck.

Kyle loved his mother and was utterly grateful for her efforts in teaching him to dance, but he had to confess that the method he had mastered at the Vennie Dexter School of Dance came in a distant second to Debbie's method.

As if the moment was not magical enough, the sentiment of the song began to fill the room.

"I bless the day I found you, I want to stay around you, and so I beg you, let it be me."

Kyle was living in a movie. Everything was perfect – the lighting, the script, the background music, the cast of characters. And the plot was developing wonderfully.

Kyle Dexter, romantic at heart, longing for love, aching for acceptance, finds himself in the arms of a beautiful woman whose heart, for years, has been bent toward his. On a darkened dance floor their hands touch. Their eyes melt into each other's, their hearts are exchanged, they profess their never dying devotion in tender words of love, and they spend the rest of the movie, and their lives, in happiness and love together.

The magic of the moment continued.

"Don't take this heaven from one, if you must cling to someone, now and forever, let it be me."

Kyle could feel the warmth of Debbie's cheek a fraction of an inch from his own. With all his heart he longed to lay his cheek against hers, but he realized the implications of such intimacy. It would be like asking her to trade discs; it would be like saying, "I love you." Was he really ready to marry Debbie and support her and their family?

The Everly Brothers supplied the answer to Kyle's question.

"So never leave me lonely, tell me you love me only, and that you'll always, let it be me."

Kyle eased his cheek against Debbie's and the softness and warmth were electrifying. Sensing that Kyle was no longer a candidate for membership in the Girl Haters Club, International, much less a candidate for president, Debbie drew Kyle more snugly into her embrace and held him there.

In that instant, Kyle Dexter's emotional Christmas list was fulfilled: tenderness, affection, acceptance, and love, all wrapped up in the beautiful package that he held in his arms. Kyle decided that if he died at that very moment, he would have lived, in his few years, one of the fullest and most satisfying lives ever lived.

Somewhere in the blur of the moment, the record ended. Kyle walked Debbie back to her chair. She smiled and said, "You dance very nicely."

"Thank you," Kyle said, "you do, too."

A lively song pulled the more acrobatic dancers back to the floor and Kyle returned to his place by the refreshment table. Through two more songs he stayed there, waiting for another opportunity to dance with Debbie. He was like a frozen man who had felt the warmth of fire for the first time. And he longed to move back into that invigorating circle of warmth again.

Finally, the lights were lowered and the mirrored ball began to spin. But just as Kyle moved to Debbie's chair, she rose and began to walk across the dance floor. He met her there with a smile. No bow, no rehearsed line, just "Would you dance with me again?"

"I can't," she said. "My dad just stuck his head in and waved. I've got to go."

Debbie must have seen the utter devastation on Kyle's face. She took his hand and smiled. "There will be other dances, Kyle, and other days."

She squeezed his hand and headed for the exit. Halfway there, she felt a touch on her elbow. Kyle was there beside her, smiling. "See you on Monday?" he asked.

"See you Monday." And Kyle's newly discovered vision of beauty walked into the night.

It was ten-twenty, ten minutes before the dance ended. Kyle sat in one of the folding chairs and beamed contentment. Not only had the night not been a disaster, it had instead been the greatest night of his life. He munched one last Christmas cookie and watched the other boys and girls dance.

Against her wishes, Nadine and Ron had stayed for the entire dance. As she was bidding farewell to some of the guests, Ron made his way to the disc jockey and whispered in his ear.

It was ten-twenty-five and time for the last dance. The disc jockey tapped on the microphone before he spoke.

"May I have your attention, please? Would everyone please clear the dance floor?" After a few moments, the dance floor was empty.

"The last dance of the night will be kicked off by two special people, two people who worked long and hard to make this dance happen. I give you the Belle of the Ball and her Prince Charming, Nadine and Ron Davis!"

The crowd clapped, the lights were lowered and the mirrored ball began to twirl. As Ron led the dumbfounded Nadine to the dance floor, strains of Percy Faith's "Theme from a Summer Place" filled the parish hall.

"Go Mr. and Mrs. Davis," several girls called out.

"Go Mom and Dad," Glinda yelled, and everyone laughed.

Ron led Nadine into the sea of dancing lights; then he took her in his arms and they danced. Everyone watched and wondered as he whispered in her ear. They watched the couple stare into each other's eyes for the longest time. Then Nadine laid her head on her Prince Charming's shoulder; and as they slowly moved to the music, she closed her eyes and smiled.

THE BIRD IN THE SNOW

Kyle Dexter lay on the living room couch and pulled the thick afghan beneath his chin. The room was cooling quickly since the space heater had been lowered to its nighttime level, but Kyle had no complaints; he loved the cold when he could snuggle to get warm.

The Dexter house was sleeping, except for Kyle. It was almost midnight, Wednesday, December 21st, 1960. In a few more minutes it would be December 22nd and Christmas would be one day closer to coming.

To Kyle Dexter, December was the ice cream on top of the cake, and Christmas morning was the chocolate syrup on top of the ice cream. Days did not get more delicious than Christmas Day, and the sweet anticipation of its coming was half the fun.

Kyle lay in the cool, darkened room, the Christmas tree lights glowing softly in the corner. They provided just enough illumination so that every detail of the room could be discerned. The piles of presents beneath the tree; the familiar family ornaments that Ricky and Donna and Kyle had carefully placed; the glistening tinsel that hung from every branch; the pine boughs that Mrs. Dexter had arranged on the bookshelf; the tray of Christmas candy that one of the widow ladies in the church had made. And quietly, so as not to wake the resting family, soothing Christmas music filled the room from the Dexter's new Zenith, high-fidelity, upright, dual-cabinet stereo system.

As the Roger Waggoner Chorale sang "Silent Night", Kyle slipped deep into the heart and soul of Christmas. Their arrangement of the classic carol beautifully mixed "Silent Night" with unmistakable strains of "Brahms' Lullaby". When he heard the song played in daylight hours, Kyle had to fight back the tears at its beauty. But on this night, with no one to see, he gave up the fight.

The mental picture of Mary cooing a lullaby over her newborn son was too much for Kyle, and the lens of his tears diffused the lights on the Christmas tree into a kaleidoscopic splash of colors.

The days since the Christmas dance were the beginning of a new and exciting chapter in Kyle's life. There was no denying it – he was in love! The

Sunday after the dance had plodded along as lazily as sorghum syrup on a winter morning. Kyle watched the clock as it painfully marked the hours that must pass before he saw Debbie again.

And on Monday morning, there she was. Had she, like him, felt the exquisite sensations in her stomach? Did she, like him, resent the hours that filled the day without him in it? Had she, like him, been changed into a different person by that one lush interlude on the dance floor?

When Debbie walked into 4-A on Monday morning and immediately looked at Kyle and smiled, he knew that his dream had come true. All that he felt for her, she felt for him as well.

That day at lunch, Kyle bought two Dreamsicles instead of his usual one. He casually walked by the girls' table and placed one beside Debbie's tray. As he walked on, he could hear the girls who saw him giggling and making silly noises. But Kyle didn't care; it was part of the price you pay when you're in love.

Kyle, however, was not satisfied with a Dreamsicle romance. His love was so much deeper and more beautiful than the amazing mixture of orange sherbet and vanilla ice cream. If he was going to show his love for Debbie, he would do it right.

Benjie and Betty were the 4-A trendsetters in all things romantic. One Monday in September they both showed up for school wearing shiny silver discs around their necks. But if you looked closely, you noticed that Benjie was wearing a disc that had "Betty" neatly engraved on it while Betty's disc proudly proclaimed "Benjie."

From that day on, "trading discs" was the pinnacle of romantic commitment for the fourth-grade classes of Raguet Elementary. Soon after that, Kyle had walked to town with three weeks of allowance in his pocket and purchased a disc for himself at Kennedy's Jewelry Store. For weeks after that, it had stayed on top of his dresser in the little velvet-lined box it came in.

But on Tuesday, Kyle wore his disc for the first time. He waited all day for the right moment. When Debbie walked to the water fountain during recess, he quickly joined her there. Before he died of nervousness, he asked her, "Will you trade discs with me?" There was no reason for his nervousness. Debbie smiled, slipped off her disc and handed it to Kyle, and Kyle did the same for Debbie.

The new arrangement was the topic of conversation in 4-A for the rest of the day. And Kyle didn't mind at all the whispers and giggles and looks from the others. He was in love, and he didn't care who knew it.

Wednesday was the best school day of the year – the day before Christmas Break! Mrs. Hartsfield had Christmas music playing on a record player when her students arrived. The day would be over by noon and there was no school work scheduled, only an endless procession of coloring pages. When one was finished, it was thumb-tacked to the bulletin board and another was begun.

At about ten o'clock a group of mothers arrived with punch and cookies and candy. The punch was served in Santa Clause mugs, and the class cheered when it was announced that they could take the mugs home. An hour later, Mrs. Hartsfield opened her presents from her devoted students. Every present she opened, it seemed, was "just what she always wanted." And then it was time to leave.

"I'll see you next year," Debbie whispered to Kyle as she prepared to leave. Kyle realized for the first time that it would be 1961 before he saw Debbie again, that countless hours in countless days would march by before he saw that beautiful smile once more.

Kyle snuggled on the couch and remembered Debbie's smile and how her eyes glistened with emotion when she looked at him. He reached for the disc on his chest and held it tightly in his fist as if to remind himself that it was all real and not just another creation of his active imagination.

With the assurance of Debbie's love in his hand and the soothing music of the season all around him, Kyle drifted off into a most peaceful and inviting world of sleep.

Kyle was awakened from his sleep by an unfamiliar sound. He was still on the couch. The record player had long since shut off, and in the silence of the night, something had nudged him awake.

It was not the kind of heart-thumping, cold-sweat, arm-thrashing awakening that Kyle had experience before, like when his cat had jumped on his head during the night. In fact, it was so different from that experience that Kyle found himself lying there, eyes opened, wondering what it was he had heard.

As he lay there, he was surprised to discover that he was still hearing the sound, a soothing whisper just beyond the living room window. It was as if the night had laid a finger to its lips and called the world to silence with an enormous, elongated "SSSSSSHHHHHHHH".

From where he lay, Kyle could see the lighted clock on the kitchen wall. It was 2:00 a.m. He had rested his head on the arm of the couch for the past two hours, and his neck and back were stiff and sore as he set up. Moving to the living room window, Kyle lifted one of the wooden slats of the Venetian blinds and looked out into the front yard.

He immediately discovered why the sound that had awakened him was such an unfamiliar one. It was snowing - in Nacogdoches! Huge, fluffy flakes were falling so thick and fast that they actually made a gentle rustling sound as they covered the darkened world. That was the sound that woke him.

As fast as he could, Kyle dressed and slipped out into a scene, the likes of which, he had only encountered in the movies. Every familiar step along Park Street seemed new and bright. Were those the same trees he walked among each day? Were those the same houses and yards he saw so often in the harsh light of day? No; the whole world had been transformed in a single hour into a magical, crystalline reproduction of its former, humdrum self.

Kyle was the only person stirring on Park Street. It was, after all, 2:00 a.m. His footsteps left the only marks in the snowy canvas for miles around, and he was careful not to deface the Currier and Ives moment any more than necessary.

He walked to the middle of the huge, open lot beside the church. Looking up into the translucent night, Kyle watched the millions, billions, trillions of fluffy flakes drifting to the world around him. Gently, silently the flakes settled around him, so thickly they fell that his recent path through the snow was almost completely obscured when he turned to look on it again.

The juxtaposition of the Christmas music that was still ringing in his ears and the silently falling flakes brought a line of poetry to Kyle's mind that fit so perfectly with the moment that he began to whisper it over and over to himself: "How silently, how silently the wondrous gift is given."

If his classmates had known of the powdery enchantment that lay just beyond their bedroom windows, they would have, without exception, run into the night to officially accept the gift. But it had fallen so softly, so silently that even their vigilant parents were missing it altogether. How silently, how silently the wondrous gift is given.

The similarity to Christmas was all too obvious. The slumbering residents of Kyle's world were so caught up in the rabid seasonal flurry of parties and shopping and concerts and shopping and travel and shopping that they were on the verge of completely missing the Greatest of Gifts, so wonderfully and silently given.

Kyle determined that this year, even if he had to wander alone through the magic of Christmas, that he would savor every morsel and consciously feel every tingling flake of the season on his upturned, rapturous face.

The beauty of the night and the wonder of the season were almost too much for Kyle to bear. Shivering from the cold yet warmed in his heart, Kyle Dexter retraced his quickly disappearing footsteps to the comfort of his own bedroom.

The pile of quilts on his bed was as cold as the night, but Kyle knew a trick. He pulled the covers over his head and captured his warm breath for a moment or two until he was warm and snug. With the assurance that the snow would be there when he awoke, Kyle drifted to sleep once more.

Kyle woke with a smile on his lips. Blue skies, no school, and a snow-covered world–what a combination! Without waiting for breakfast, Kyle rushed into the thickly wooded lot behind his house to explore the brilliant miracle before it melted into memory.

He waded deep into the shrubs and trees, but no matter where he went, the snow had been there before him. In an open patch ahead of him, Kyle saw hundreds of black objects against the white carpet of snow. They bounced and hopped and chirped, a massive flock of blackbirds looking in the snow for one of the rare items on the winter menu.

They must have sensed Kyle's presence. In a unified explosion of fluttering, the flock beat its way into the sky and out of sight, in search of a less boy-infested environment.

Kyle was sorry to see them leave. He was half-way through mouthing the words, "You don't have to leave; I would never hurt you," when he was caught up short. But he had hurt them! He was, and there was no denying it, a bird-killer. Why shouldn't they be afraid; why shouldn't they fly away?

If there was one memory that could darken a brilliant day, it was the still clear memory of the wounded robin biting at the barrel of the bb-gun, finally lying still and bloodied after Kyle's murderous deed.

Once this memory had intruded upon his otherwise delightful day, Kyle turned for home. With the purity of the morning spoiled, he began to retrace his steps when a movement in the snow captured his attention. Five hundred black dots had risen from the snow, but one had remained behind.

When he drew near, Kyle discovered that one bird was alone in the snow after all the others had left, and upon closer examination, the reason for his staying behind was clear. When the bird had landed, its head had slipped between the prongs of a v-shaped twig and, through some unfortunate twists and ill-advised turns, the bird had caused the twigs to pinch his neck and hold him firmly in the snow.

The frightened bird struggled more and more as the large stranger drew near. As his struggling continued, the bird was eventually lying unnaturally on his side, buried half-way in the snow. With Kyle standing directly over him, the bird, apparently resigned to his fate, ceased to struggle.

It was clear to Kyle that the bird would not survive for long if buried in the snow. He quickly removed the scarf his mother had placed around his neck and wrapped it around the bird's body, over and over until only his head could be seen. Then Kyle carefully separated the prongs of the twig and lifted the bird in his hands.

"Whatcha got there?" his mother asked as Kyle walked through the back door.

"A bird", Kyle answered; "I'm going to warm him up by the stove."

Kyle explained how he came to be holding a full-grown blackbird as his mother listened with amazement.

"And so I brought him in here to let him rest and get warm before I turned him loose."

"He's beautiful", his mother said as she gently stroked the bird's head with her finger.

"Look how his feathers shine!" Depending on how the bird turned his head, the feathers that once appeared solid black shone in a brilliant purple hue instead.

"And look how he's looking at you! It's almost like he knows you saved him from the snow."

The bird turned his head one way and another, but always looking at Kyle. It was as if he knew his life was literally in Kyle's hands, and so he was sizing up the creature that held him, for good or ill.

Kyle stroked the bird's head and held him so the space heater warmed them both.

After a few minutes, Kyle announced, "I'm going to let him go now." Mrs. Dexter gave the bird's head one last gentle touch and held the door open for Kyle.

He walked slowly back to the clearing, enjoying every moment of holding such a wild and beautiful manifestation of life in his hands.

"All right," Kyle said, slowing unwrapping the scarf, "let's see how you do."

Kyle peeled off layer after layer of scarf, and more and more bird appeared as he did. Finally, he dropped the scarf to the ground and held only the bird in his hands. The small black body was soft and warm to the touch, making it difficult for Kyle to consider letting him go. After stroking his head a few more precious times, Kyle let the bird stand on his left hand and removed his right hand altogether.

For a wonderfully prolonged moment, the bird stood on his hand and looked him over again, turning his head this way and that, looking at him, it seemed to Kyle, squarely in the eye. Then he spread his wings and was off to find the flock.

Kyle watched the bird disappear from sight and turned slowly for home and warmth and a late breakfast. His way home led him uncomfortably close to the shrub in which he had killed the robin months before. Since that time, Kyle had steered clear of the place in an effort to avoid the painful memories associated with it. He had always imagined, if he entered the place again, that the bloodied body of the robin would still be there, a perpetual reproach, indelible evidence of his shameful act.

But on this day, drawn by an unmistakable tugging at his heart, Kyle entered the shrub. The lack of greenery made it easier for him to gain the clearing in the center. And when he got there, only pure, untrampled whiteness covered the ground. The evidence of his crime had long been washed away, and a new, clean canopy of snow had replaced it.

Kyle began to contemplate the blackbird he saved from the snow and held in his hands. He knew that saving one bird did not make up for the fact that he had killed another. He intuitively understood that there was no Great Scale where evil deeds could be balanced with a sufficient number of good ones. He knew with complete certainty that even saving a thousand birds could not expunge the awful deed that weighed so heavily upon him. But before him, in the snow, was a picture of what might. A picture of forgiveness.

Kyle had heard the words in church, but he always thought they applied to criminals and gangsters. "Though your sins are like scarlet, they shall be as white as snow." Now he knew differently. In the silence of this frozen temple, with a choir of birds around him and a grove of suppliants lifting their branches in praise, Kyle understood that forgiveness was offered to him as well.

Even though he shared the thought with no one, Kyle was convinced that the blackbird had been a messenger from God, that it had drawn him to a place he would never have chosen to go, and had offered, in his trusting gaze, a message of grace and renewal.

It was with light steps that Kyle made his way home through the snow. There was such a burden lifted from his soul that he was surprised that his feet made any impression in the snow at all. Forgiveness had been offered to him in indisputable terms, and Kyle Dexter had accepted it as readily as a ship-wrecked man accepts a glass of cool, fresh water.

"Watcha thinkin'", Vennie Dexter asked as she did so many times of Kyle. "You look like something's about to explode inside you. Something good, I hope."

"Do you remember, Mom, when we were at that piano recital and I asked you if something could mean something else, something more?"

"I'll never forget that day."

"Well, I was just thinking today that maybe….maybe just about everything means something more. Maybe every bird and every flake of snow and every friendly smile means something more and something big, and maybe every time we do something right or do something wrong or don't do something we later wish we did do, maybe all those times mean something more and something important; maybe everything, every little thing means something more, something that will last forever. Does that make any sense at all?"

Vennie Dexter turned the sizzling bacon for Kyle's breakfast and smiled.

"I think you may be on to something, Kyle; and I think it's going to take you exactly one lifetime to figure it all out. Now go get out of your wet clothes and get ready for breakfast."

Kyle looked out the French doors once more before he headed for his room. The crisp air, the blue sky, the sparkling snow, the nearness of Christmas, the wonder of love given and accepted and returned, the family he cherished, a clean slate with life – it all added up for Kyle into the perfect blend of a settled past, an exciting present, and a limitless future.

Kyle looked at his own reflection in the glass door. The eyes that looked back seemed more brimful of hope and tranquility than they ever had, and the prospect of a new year with all its uncertainty seemed to lose every shred of dread it once held.

Kyle smiled and whispered, quietly, but with great conviction, "Hey world, bring on 1961; Kyle Dexter is ready for it!"

With the smell of bacon urging him on, Kyle ran up the stairs, two at a time, changed from his wet clothes and got ready for the rest of his life.

ACKNOWLEDGEMENTS

It is a daunting task to recognize and thank all who have helped to bring this literary journey to its first destination – publication. But as daunting a task as it is, I would feel most ungrateful if I did not try.

Thanks, first of all, to Kimberly Verhines at SFA Press for seeing something in my manuscript worthy of consideration, and to Jerri Bourrous for patiently editing it into its present form.

Thanks also to Anita, my best friend and wife of 40 years, for being an amazing mother to our five extraordinary children, my first and most valued reader, and the most gentle of critics. She has blanketed our family with love and our marriage with relentless grace. The smile that I almost universally wear is largely because of her.

And for this story, thanks most of all to Nacogdoches, Texas and the incomparable cast of characters I met there. I could not possibly list all the wonderful friendships that began there, all the teachers and mentors who poured their lives into mine, all the experiences, both blissful and painful, that molded me into the man I am today. The members of First Christian Church get top billing in that cast of characters. So many of those saints have taken their final bow on this stage, but the lines they spoke and the lives they lived before me will never be forgotten. Finally, I am honored to be a son and brother in a truly remarkable family. Special thanks to my sister, Donna, for allowing herself to be featured in my story.

Like so many in today's mobile society, I have lived in numerous cities and states. But as the decades pass, I have discovered over and over that no matter where I am, my heart and mind and values always find their center in Nacogdoches, Texas. I therefore, forever and unashamedly, declare myself to be a Son of Nacogdoches, and it is to its fine people that I humbly dedicate this book.

CPSIA information can be obtained
at www.ICGtesting.com
Printed in the USA
LVOW03s1006191017
552932LV00003B/11/P